PENG

JUST FOR YOU

Rahul Saini is the bestselling author of four hugely popular novels—
Those Small Lil Things, *Just Like in the Movies*, *The Orange Hangover*
and *Paperback Dreams*. Formerly an architect, he has a keen interest
in photography, filmmaking and fine arts. Currently, he serves as a
visiting faculty member for an art and design programme at a prestigious
university in India. He takes an active interest in the welfare of his
students.

From the small Punjabi town of Jalandhar, he is a high-spirited
young man who spends much of his time travelling, mostly to parts of
Himachal Pradesh. He loves spending time with his family and friends.

Praise for *Paperback Dreams*

'Decidedly light-hearted—it will have you chuckling'—*Telegraph*

'A tongue-in-cheek fictional account of publishing in India'—*The Hindu*

By the same author

Paperback Dreams

JUST *for* YOU

RAHUL SAINI

Penguin
metro reads

PENGUIN METRO READS
Published by the Penguin Group
Penguin Books India Pvt. Ltd, 7th Floor, Infinity Tower C, DLF Cyber City,
Gurgaon 122 002, Haryana, India
Penguin Group (USA) Inc., 375 Hudson Street, New York, New York 10014, USA
Penguin Group (Canada), 90 Eglinton Avenue East, Suite 700, Toronto, Ontario,
M4P 2Y3, Canada
Penguin Books Ltd, 80 Strand, London WC2R 0RL, England
Penguin Ireland, 25 St Stephen's Green, Dublin 2, Ireland (a division of
Penguin Books Ltd)
Penguin Group (Australia), 707 Collins Street, Melbourne, Victoria 3008, Australia
Penguin Group (NZ), 67 Apollo Drive, Rosedale, Auckland 0632, New Zealand
Penguin Books (South Africa) (Pty) Ltd, Block D, Rosebank Office Park,
181 Jan Smuts Avenue, Parktown North, Johannesburg 2193, South Africa

Penguin Books Ltd, Registered Offices: 80 Strand, London WC2R 0RL, England

First published in Penguin Metro Reads by Penguin Books India 2014

ISBN 9780143421429

Typeset in Adobe Garamond by R. Ajith Kumar, New Delhi
Printed at Thomson Press India Ltd, New Delhi

A PENGUIN RANDOM HOUSE COMPANY

'I love the sound of applause, even if I have to buy it.'

—Sugar Motta
Glee, 'Heart' (S03 E13)

'If you can love someone with your whole heart, even one person, then there's salvation in life. Even if you can't get together with that person.'

—Haruki Murakami
1Q84

Prologue

I need one more glass of my favourite cocktail—a mojito!

It's really, really hot and my throat is parched. Around me I can see people heading out to the beach. Nisha and I are lying on our super comfortable lounging chairs with our cocktails by our sides and our legs stretched all the way to the sea. There is a cool breeze blowing but it gets extremely hot when it's still.

Nisha is lying under the umbrella beside me, eyes closed in a blissful sleep. Her white bikini top and the light, printed chiffon skirt leave little to the imagination. I stare at her cleavage with mounting desire.

'What?' she asks, suddenly opening her eyes and smiling.

'Nothing. Just wondering whether I should ask for another mojito or just forget about it and jump to plan B,' I say, winking.

'Don't you be getting any ideas now!' she says and closes her eyes again.

I lean back in my chair again, the blue sea merging into the sky like a giant canvas. I sigh with relief. Goa is beautiful but the best part is the luxury. Life is not for the weak. It's for those who have the strength to grab things in their own hands. It's for those who know how to live and enjoy themselves. It's for those who . . . wait! What is this warm heavy thing on my lap? What is this . . . flat hard surface? Why does it feel different around me? What's going on?

I feel my lap and find my laptop there. And then my eyes are open. In the dim morning light I can make out the walls of my shabby room. Damn! It was all a dream! I fell asleep as I was struggling to write the ending for the chapter I was writing. Damn! Damn!

1

He is a writer and he just can't write today with his girlfriend sleeping by his side—Rohit

This is not how it's supposed to be! I am an author. I am supposed to have a super sharp mind that works at lightning speed and create plots and stories like nobody's business. I should have submitted this manuscript long ago, taken an insanely hefty advance and spent my time after that reclining on a beach with my girlfriend wearing funky shades, with clear blue skies and sparkling waters around us like in my dream. Instead, I'm sitting on my bed in my pyjamas on a Saturday afternoon, wracking my brains to find a way for the story to progress, while my girlfriend naps by my side.

I *have* the story, the cosmic energies have sent it to me; I can sense it, I can *feel* it! The story needs to be told—it needs to be born. It is destined. I must not panic. I am only an instrument in its creation that is just a bit jammed right now. Maybe that's a sign from the cosmic lords telling me that I need to take a break, that I need to rest.

I reach out to turn off my computer when I get an email alert. Hesitant, I click it open. I can guess who it's from and any doubts I may have had are cleared when the email opens, shining tauntingly at me from the computer screen:

```
Dear Rohit,
I hope you are in best of spirits and things
are going wonderfully at your end.
   We at Big Publisher X are eagerly waiting
for your manuscript which is due to be
submitted next month. Please consider this
a gentle reminder from us as we are really
eager to start working on the project.
   Hope to hear from you soon.
   Best,
   Wishvish Bhomba
   For Big Publisher X
```

Of course I am in the best of spirits! I am so good and pumped up with energy that . . . I am so . . . *jammed*!

I quickly send them an email saying that I am feeling *superb* and will be submitting the manuscript next month as planned and end with a smiley.

Finally turning off my laptop, I put it on the table by the bed and turn to Nisha. She looks at me with her puffy, sleepy eyes. Holding my hand, she kisses it gently and asks, 'What happened?'

My Nisha, my love—she is the one person who has always

helped me sail through tough times. I put my arm around her and kiss her shoulder.

'Nothing. It's . . . I know what I want to write but . . . the words just won't come. I just can't seem to write! I'm so frustrated.'

'Don't worry. It'll happen. Creativity takes time. You cannot force it,' Nisha says as she sits up, leaning against the headboard.

'I know, I know . . . and I have a really good story this time! Fiction based on the lives of real people is the next big thing and I am writing on the life of India's bestselling novelist, Vikram Rawat. *The Paperback King*, that's what I'm going to call it, since he literally rules the market. What do you think?'

Nisha smiles encouragingly.

'It's been really exciting to work on the story and do all the research. I am actually tracing his life and figuring out how he became a writer. It's all really cool! At times I feel like one of those snooty intellectual writers whom we see on TV or at high-profile, large-scale literary festivals.'

Nisha looks at me admiringly. 'Don't stress so much. Just keep working on it,' she says, twisting her long, black hair into a bun. She is wearing one of my white gunjies and I love how she looks in them—shabby and sexy at the same time, like one of those actresses in Hollywood action flicks.

'What?' she says as she notices me staring.

'Nothing.' I smile, roll over to her and take her in my arms. 'It's just that . . . at times I think sitting at home all the time is what's not working for me. Like you go out to work and are at home only on Saturdays and Sundays whereas I am here all week long. Every day. I don't even go out much any more. My last job was awful and I had this *terrible, terrible* boss but still it used to give me some kind of inspiration. I think I need people around me to inspire me, I need activity and movement around me.'

I had a regular job till a few months back teaching fine arts to undergraduate students. It was really good for me but there was this evil, fat, alien-like boss because of whom I had to quit.

At times I feel that I am really lost, that my sad, insignificant life is not going anywhere. I am going to turn thirty soon and if I really think about it, what have I achieved so far? Just a few novels under my name and nothing else? I studied fine arts, but I am not really working towards becoming a serious artist. I started teaching but I quit that job. Where am I headed and what am I doing with my life? I know I want to become a writer but what if that does not work out? At times I begin to panic about growing older and the fact that all my other friends are doing so well for themselves. Did I start my career a bit too late? Look at all the other authors of popular fiction we have these days—they are all younger than me. I am like this old loser trying to keep up with them. Anyway, now is probably not the best time to think about it since I'm writing a new novel.

'You want to eat something? I am hungry,' I ask Nisha as we climb out of the bed.

'Yeah, I think I could snack up a little,' she says as she stretches.

'Great. Then we can have Maggi. I'll go make some,' I say.

I am in the kitchen chopping onions for the noodles when I hear the doorbell ring.

An excited Pranav is at the door. 'Sir-ji! You have no idea what is happening in college!' He grabs me by my shoulders, turns me around and walks in with me.

'What?' I ask.

'Wait, let me show you. I have some pictures.' He pulls out his phone from his pocket.

Pranav had been one of my students when I was teaching in college. He was going through some troubled times back then, before he came to live with us—a long story that I am not going to get into right now.

He gives me his phone and I look at the pictures he wants me to see. I am amazed—almost shocked actually—by what I see. There are students sitting in the corridors of the college building where I used to teach, holding boards and placards saying things like: 'WE WANT OUR TEACHER BACK' and 'NO ROHIT SIR, NO CLASSES'. I am speechless. The kids genuinely want me back. It's all very flattering; I'm so moved by their actions.

'I am going get you back in the college, sir-ji!' Pranav says enthusiastically.

'It is really nice to know, Pranav, that you guys want me back as your teacher but there is no way that I'm coming back.'

'What, sir-ji!' he says making a face.

'I have too much self-esteem,' I say, 'I cannot go back to work there.'

'Please, sir-ji, don't be so dramatic! We want you back and we are getting you back. That's it!'

It's a very nice feeling to know that someone wants you so much but there is seriously no way I am going back. These kids who want me to return don't really need me now. I have taught them everything I had to. I almost feel like saying 'I won't come back now because I stay only as long as you need me and leave when you want me' just like in the movies but I don't. I am not going back; I am sure of that. But for a moment I understand why I am where I am.

2

Great sex and success . . . some authors have it all!
—Jeet

I stretch lazily and slide away from under the white satin covers that are warm from the heat of our semi-naked bodies. I walk to the floor-to-ceiling window through which the golden light of the morning sun is entering the room. The rays of the sun are warm as they touch my shoulders and my chest. I turn around and look at Neeti. She is sleeping peacefully on the bed. It was quite an event last evening: the launch of our third book together. Writing and releasing a new novel every six months is not easy. And it's even more difficult to go on these promotional tours. I turn my gaze out of the window again and look at the expansive cityscape. Our hotel room is on the eighth floor and offers a great view of a major part of the city. Being in Bangalore always makes me happy. I used to love coming here for the events when my first novel was released. It's funny how time flies, how we have grown from authors whom nobody knew to the authors everyone is talking about.

There is a soft knock on the door. I open the door and see the bellboy with the day's newspaper in his hand. He smiles and hands it to me.

The papers must have covered our last evening's launch. I go and sit on the chair next to the window, pull out the magazine section of the newspaper and see a huge half-page spread about our launch with a cute picture of Neeti and me holding our book.

YOUNG WRITERS ROCK!

We keep seeing launches and events but not many are as loved and lively as those of Jeet and Neeti. The writing super duo was in the city again and had a rocking launch for their new book, *As Long as You Live with Me, I Will Be Alive.* This is their third book since they began collaborating as writers a year and a half ago and is already topping the national bestseller list. Youngsters all over the country love the writing duo; in fact, Jeet Obiroi has become the heart-throb of thousands of young girls in every city in India. Last evening they went crazy trying to catch a glimpse of him.

I am still reading the article when I notice Neeti stirring under the soft white covers. She is up, I know. This is how she wakes up. She rolls over to one side, then to the other and then back to the first side, and rubs her face with her hands like a child after waking up and sitting up in bed.

'Good morning,' I look at her and smile.

'Morning,' she smiles back and gets off the bed, walks up to me, puts her hand on my chest and gives me a warm, long kiss.

'They have covered yesterday's event quite well.'

'Let me see,' she takes the paper from my hands and starts to read. 'Nice!'

'Isn't it a little funny? Only a year and a half of working together and we have already finished five manuscripts. Out of which the three that have been published have become huge successes.' I look at her.

'I know. Isn't that amazing?' She comes and sits on my lap and runs her hand on my abs.

'Absolutely!' I slide my hand under the loose T-shirt she is wearing and caress her back. 'And it feels so great.'

She nods, 'Yes, I can feel it under my thigh,' aware that I am getting a boner.

I grin and we kiss again. It's a long and warm kiss. I caress her back as she pulls me towards her and arches her back. We look deeply into each other's eyes with burning passion. I do not want her to stop; I want her to touch me and run her hands all over me. I tug the T-shirt off her and hug her tight. I like mornings as a rule; I like them even better when they start with sex.

3

Some people reach their late twenties and have never had a sex chat in their life . . . until now—Rohit

We live in a funny age. It's so tough to get any work done at all these days! There are so, so, so many distractions! For the past three days I have only managed to write a sorry eight hundred words—that is just like two and a half pages—when I should have finished at least two chapters. I stare at the Word doc on my computer screen and am totally blank. All I want to do is go to IMDB.com and check which new movie trailers are out and see what everyone's up to on Facebook. I think the generations before us were so lucky from this point of view. The number of things you could do in life were limited back then, no doubt about it; but man, there were hardly any distractions! It must have been so easy to *focus*! Look at my state right now: it is so pathetic. I have been in bed the whole morning forcing myself to write but all I have done is check my Facebook notifications after every ten minutes and like and post lame comments on others' pictures like 'Hey! Nice pic dude. Didn't know you went to Kerala' and see how many likes I got on the picture of my last visit to Mcleodganj that I uploaded yesterday. My best picture ever on Facebook got a record number of likes: 348. All I am wondering now is if this one will cross that figure and touch the godly total of five hundred likes? It is definitely not a good day for me to work. I think I should take the day off (like I have been doing for the past week now).

I close the document I am working on and my eyes hypnotically go to the 'turn on chat' button at the right bottom of the Facebook page. I do not go online to chat generally. I used to at one time but then I stopped. I have so many readers on my page and sometimes they ask the weirdest personal questions. It generally starts with very simple, innocent ones like how many brothers or sisters I have or and which city I live in or if I am a full-time writer now or have another job. But after that the awkward part starts: Are you single or committed? How many girlfriends do you have? Are you seeing anyone, and, many times, how often do you have sex with her? But for some reason, I want to go online today. And maybe I want to be asked personal questions right now—I think that might make me think a bit about what my personal life is like right now and help me reflect about it.

Facebook chat shows 428 of my friends online but none of them are my real friends. Maybe I'll just wait for someone to ping me, I decide, staring on my laptop screen as I drum my fingers on the panel. After a few awkward seconds, a chat window pops up.

Saima: Hi!

I peer at the tiny display picture in the window—she looks pretty.

Rohit: Hey!
Saima: What's up?
Rohit: Nothing. Was just working. Thought of taking a break.
Saima: Cool! How has your day been so far?
Rohit: Good. How was yours?

This is going good, I think, *basic chat.*

Saima: Mine was really HOT and SEXY!
Rohit: Oh, you mean like you had a great day.
Saima: LOL! No. I mean hot and sexy like HOT and SEXY.
Rohit: Oh.
Saima: Yeah, just had sex with my boyfriend.

What?! What am I supposed to say to that?

Rohit: Good, that is very . . . good.
Saima: You bet it was! You know I am so good in bed that my boyfriend calls me THE GIRL FULL OF SEX.

Oh God!

Rohit: Okay . . .that's nice to know.

Oh my God! What is wrong with this girl! Why is she talking like this?

Saima: LOL! You sound shocked. Am I shocking you?

Yes!

Rohit: No, not at all. Not at all, why would you say that?
Saima: Oh come on! It is so obvious. You are taking such long pauses.
Rohit: No no. That's not so.
Saima: LOL! Okay. You know something? This picture that you see, it's not my real picture.
Rohit: Oh. OK.

That's totally normal. People use other people's pictures as their display pictures all the time.

Saima: You want to see my real picture?
Rohit: Sure.

Within seconds, a picture of a set of female breasts appear on my laptop screen!

Saima: Do you like the real me?

Oh my God, this is a sex chat! She is sex chatting with me!!! I have never done this in my entire life before!

Rohit: Yeah it's nice.

What am I supposed to say???!!!! How does one sex chat???

Saima: Only nice?

What do I say? WHAT DO I SAY?

Saima: You don't like me ☹
Rohit: No, no. you are nice.
Saima: No. You don't like the real me.
Rohit: No, no. I do . . . I really like the real you.

This is really awkward for me. I have never sex chatted before . . . and I truly believe that everyone should experience such things at least once in life. And you know, for me this is more like research. What if I have to write a sex chat in one of my books some time? How will I know what to write then? How will I know what a sex chat is like? This is my chance to learn!

Still, I can't help wonder that who the hell this girl is and how I could have added her to my friends' list. I don't accept all the friend requests I get. Those who send me a friend request should either have a substantial number of friends in common with me or a genuine interest in my writing.

Saima: Then say something about the real me ☺

Just think and type, just think and type something nice about her breasts.

Rohit: The real you is very beautiful. The real you has skin that looks smooth and beautiful and dusky. The real you is beautifully round and supple and one can't help but feel the desire to touch and hold the beautiful real you.
Saima: LOL! You are so funny. You are so nerdy. But I like the nerdy you. I like you. LOL!
Rohit: Thank you ☺

It is kind of flattering what she is saying.

Saima: Do you want to see more of the real me?

Oh my God, she is a nymphomaniac! A sex addict!!!

I am struggling to think of what I should say when the doorbell rings.

Rohit: Hey, gtg! Someone's here.
Saima: LOL! You going to wank, aren't you? You horny little nerdy beast!
Rohit: No, no. someone's here. Honestly!
Saima: OK ☺ I believe my horny little nerdy beast.
Rohit: Thank you

Thank you? Seriously? Thank you???

Saima: OK. You go now. And next time we chat, I will send you more pictures of the real me. ;)
Rohit: Sure. That will be nice. Thanks. Gtg. Bye.

I go offline. *Man! She's one crazy girl!* I put my laptop aside and walk out of my room with thoughts about Saima whirling in my mind and the image of her gorgeous round boobs flashing in front of my eyes over and over again. Maybe she's not as crazy as I think she is. Maybe she was just being philosophical. Breasts are the essence of womanhood, some may think—they support life and nourish the infant. Maybe that is why she sent me a picture of her breasts. Maybe I am just fantasizing about the whole thing. Maybe I am the sex-driven, dirty pervert here.

I open the door and find Nisha standing in front of me.

'Hey! How was your day?' I ask as she comes and dumps her bag on the side table lazily and crashes on the sofa.

'It was okay. The same as every day. What could be new?' she sighs. 'How was yours?'

There is no way I'm telling her that I had a little sex chat with one of my Facebook friends!

'It was okay.' I shrug, sit next to her on the sofa and put my arm around her shoulder. She looks exhausted right now, tired after a whole day's work but the fragrance of her watermelon lip balm is really tempting. Watermelon is my favourite fruit. I hold her and kiss her and want to keep kissing her forever. We share a long passionate kiss and then she pulls back and smiles at me, 'God! What's gotten into you today?'

'Love, only love.' I say in a deep husky voice, sounding like a cheesy hero in some old romantic movie.

She laughs, rolling her eyes and pushes me away. 'Did you get any work done today? How is your writing going?'

'That is . . . not a very good question.' I fake a little cough.

'I was thinking,' she says as she gets up and walks towards our room, 'if you are facing so much trouble with your writing, why don't you take help from an editor? Hire an editorial service. That might solve your problem.'

'Hey, that's a good idea actually,' I say as I churn the idea in my mind. This might actually solve my problem. 'Yeah, I should hire one. I'll try finding one on the Internet.'

She nods. 'Do that. Where is Pranav? Isn't it too late for him to be out?'

'He is at his friend's place. Will be staying there for the night. Had some group assignment to finish, he said. We could do our own thing . . .' I say hinting at something more than a kiss as Nisha walks into our room.

She doesn't respond.

4

Some people never change—they remain bitter and twisted forever—Karun

Carnivore Karun: So u ditched me, ditcher. U ditched me in the middle of things and you left me.

Dicey Devika: Oh God! You smiled and you said goodbye. You were fine with it remember?

Carnivore Karun: Ya ya, whatever.

Dicey Devika: What? Your last words before I left were and I am quoting you here 'I want you to go and learn how to make movies and come back so that we can make movies and take Bollywood by a storm'.

Carnivore Karun: Ya ya. FINE! So tell me, how is the US treating you?

Dicey Devika: it's good here. Quite exciting actually. I like the people here. You can wear anything and go out and no one will even turn around to look at you.

Carnivore Karun: So you mean you are roaming around in your bra and your panties every day and no one is bothering to look at you?

Dicey Devika: Shut up!

Carnivore Karun: LOL! How's the film course going?

Dicey Devika: Going good actually. It's very taxing though but a lot of learning. And you know, they invite famous Hollywood stars over for guest lectures all the time. Next week we are expecting BRAD PITT!

Carnivore Karun: Wow! That is cool!

Dicey Devika: Ya, and I think the novel we wrote together also was very helpful in getting me the scholarship for this course.

Carnivore Karun: That was your game plan always, no? Get a book published with me and then get admission for this course with a full scholarship ;P

Dicey Devika: Shut up. Only you make plans like that.

Carnivore Karun: Ya ya.

Dicey Devika: Anyway. You tell me. How are things going at your end?

Carnivore Karun: Things are going great here actually. And if everything goes as planned, I will destroy Rohit within the next six months. I just need to get my hands on something and then his writing career will be over. He should never have humiliated me like that. He should never have thrown those eggs at me. Seriously man, what is he? 10? Who does that?

Dicey Devika: Karun, can I be honest with you?

Carnivore Karun: ?

Dicey Devika: I think you should focus more on improving your writing rather than spending all your energy in trying to destroy Rohit. The world is too big to concentrate on puny things like these. If your work is good people will like it anyway. You won't need to get anyone out of your way to become successful.

Carnivore Karun: :o Is this the same Devika who helped me do everything we did together? I think her chat account has been hacked!

Dicey Devika: When I look back at everything I did back then, I realize I was being immature.

Carnivore Karun: Oh please! Cut it out.

Dicey Devika: I am just trying to—

Carnivore Karun: And don't even think of starting with all that karma shit. I don't believe in any of that.

Dicey Devika: Okay. Suit yourself then.

Carnivore Karun: Rohit is competition and that is why I need to get rid of him. And in any case, my writing is quite good. Better than everyone else's. And whenever I need to write, I can just sit down and churn out my next novel, which will be some time next year. It will be done in no time.

Dicey Devika: Okay

Carnivore Karun: You better finish this course and come back quickly. Remember the pact? You write and direct and I produce. Then we take the whole industry by storm.

Dicey Devika: Yes

5

This world runs on money and one can't get anything without putting in some—one can't even get fame without it—Jeet

I glance at the dashboard clock in my car and see that I am seven minutes early for the meeting. I bring my car to a stylish screeching halt in the parking lot and step out. Striding into the building, I take the lift to the fourth floor, to the office of B-Famous, the PR firm I hired six months ago. I walk up to the reception, 'Mr Aanush is expecting me.'

The chic girl behind the desk nods, picks up the receiver of the phone, punches two of the keys and says, 'Sir, Mr Jeet Obiroi is here.'

She puts down the receiver, turns to me and says, 'You can go in.'

As I push open the door, Aanush gets up to shake hands with me. 'Hey, Jeet, come on in. I was waiting for you.'

'How are you?' I ask

'Good. Would you like to have something? Tea, coffee, juice?'

'It's okay. I am good.'

He presses a button on the intercom and says, 'Please send in water.'

'I liked the coverage that we managed for the Bangalore event. Very positive,' I say.

'Thank you, Jeet. You know what—once the media gets to know you, getting coverage becomes a lot easier.' He smiles. 'And you are quite a favourite with most of the journalists I am in touch with, especially the women.'

'Well, that is nice to know.' I cannot resist smiling back. 'You are doing a good job. I am happy with your service.' I place a white envelope containing the payment on the table.

Aanush takes the envelope, pulls the cheque out, looks at it and then says, 'Thank you. How is your new book doing? How many copies have we sold?'

'Around ten thousand copies in a week. But for all media queries, please quote a figure of twenty-two thousand copies.'

'Okay,' he nods.

'How are things going, by the way, according to you?' I ask.

'Things are good. Things are good. But I think we can do better.'

'Like how?'

'I have a feeling a controversy will help, if you guys can generate one. It will push your sales.'

'Hmm. . .' I begin to think seriously.

6

**They only want to sell their books and their ethics
can go sleep on the back seat, is what he thinks
about other authors at times—Rohit**

THE NEW SCHOOL OF AUTHORS

In the last few years, the Indian market has gone through a
major boom. Not only have the young started reading more,
but they've also started writing more. Compared to an average
release of around 100 books per month till a few years ago,
the market now gulps over 300 titles from Indian authors
every month. While the quality of the writing might send
some literary critics to their beds, shivering, spending days
in depressed slumber, the quantities sold are no less than
shocking. A fresh debut author can easily sell upwards of
30,000 copies within a month, without any major promotion
or PR activity, especially if it is a love story.

Looking at the sale figures for such books, the highest
selling author in this category is, hands down, Vikram Rawat.

Where his books have broken all sales records in India in the past few years, his new book, *The Unwanted Movement*, is being hailed as a bestseller even before its scheduled release date. Whether it will be loved or loathed by its readers is yet to be seen, but the fact is that more than four lakh copies of the book have been pre-ordered from online and offline bookstores across India.

Apart from Rawat, there are many other authors who are very popular with the young readers as well. Jeet Obiroi is another young author who is immensely popular with young readers. Obiroi has written a string of novels, each one published within months of its predecessor, and all of them hugely successful. His books sell an average of 30,000 copies every month. Another rising star in this category of writers is Karun Mukharjee. This two-book-old author seems to be the next big thing. His second novel, *My Love, My Angel is the Best Thing in My Life*, which was released earlier this year, sold 15,000 copies within weeks of its release. The content of these books may be a cause for concern for the parents of the target readership who may still be in school or college. At times the language in these books can be very explicit, such as 'I see her big boobs in front of me and want to grab and press them—pom pom!' and 'Will you squeeze my love stick? I want your hands to touch it and feel it.'

While the morals and ethics may be different, the choice of the readers and the sale figures of these books for sure tell a different story . . .

This is totally insane! I cannot read any further! I seriously wonder where this world is headed and what is wrong with today's youth? Is sex the only thing they care about? Is that all they want? The other day there was a piece on TV which claimed that 92 per cent of pop songs are about sex. *Do they never think about anything else?* This whole thing is so overrated! It's insane! The media has ruined it all! Just think about the advertising industry—they even use sex to sell juice and cold drinks! It's as if human beings came to earth only to have sex and do nothing else!

All that aside, there's not even a single mention of any of my books in the whole article? It's obvious that they are talking about only those authors who have hired PR people but still, they could have added a teeny tiny one-liner about me. God, I am such a loser! And these people, they are all younger than me. I mean besides Vikram Rawat, Jeet Obiroi is about three years younger than me and Karun is about seven years younger than me. God! I am old and . . . completely pathetic! Have I completely lost my chance in life?

I immediately go on the Internet and begin to Google the names of famous writers. George R.R. Martin started writing novels when he was around thirty, as did Murakami; Stephen King began writing when he was twenty. Even on IMDB.com, most famous actors seem to have started their careers in their late twenties. Maybe I am not in that bad a place. Maybe I just need to calm down and take a deep breath.

As always, Facebook, gmail and the Word file of my next manuscript are open on my computer. I decide to quickly check my mail once more before I start my writing for the day.

There is a mail from one of the editors I had shortlisted and sent a query to regarding editorial work:

```
Dear Rohit,
    Thank you for showing interest in We are
for the Writers. We provide excellent editing
services. The long list of the services
we provide include critical reviews and
suggestions for submitted manuscripts and
copy-editing. Our list of esteemed clients
includes major authors of our time like
Vikram Rawat, Vaibhav Sharma, Naresh Jha
and Kamal Khan. For your reference, we are
attaching a sample edit from Rawat's second
book. We look forward to hearing from you.
    Cheers,
    Subodh Sharma
```

These people sound good; maybe I can give them a try. I download and open the file Subodh has sent and quickly go through it. There is quite some work that has been done on the manuscript. There are so many changes and suggestions . . . it seems the manuscript has almost been re-written. And they have done a good job. I can definitely give them a try.

I close my mail and try to orient myself to work when a message notification pops up on my Facebook account. I click open the message and it's the sex chat girl again. Saima. '*Are you horny right now?*' the message reads. I am seriously not in the mood. I ignore the message and try to focus on my story.

I read the last few lines I had written and try to collect my thoughts when the doorbell rings. One just cannot work in today's world. *Simply cannot!*

I open the door and a super-excited Pranav dashes in.

'Check your Facebook page, sir-ji!'

'What?' Oh my God! Is he the horny girl?!! Is he the one who has been *sex* chatting with me? It was all a prank he was playing on me! Damn! This is terrible! Damn it! This is cheating! Pure cheating!!!

'Sorry. I mean mail. Check your mail,' he says.

I stare at him suspiciously as I walk to my laptop and open my mail.

'Is it there? Is the mail there?' He is literally jumping.

I see a new mail from Gurinder Singh, the principal of the college I used to teach at, and where Pranav still studies. I look at Pranav, confused; he looks back at me, his eyes popping out with excitement.

'Open it! Open the mail!'

It's an offer letter from Gurinder. He is offering me my job back.

'I told you I will get you back! I told you!' Pranav is out of control.

I look back at him and am at a loss for words.

'Now you'll return to the college and everything will be like it was before.'

I do not want to join the college again. I do not want to go back to that place. I was forced to leave by unfair means and that was the worst kind of insult I have ever been subjected to.

'Pranav, I won't accept this offer.'

'*Sir-ji! Please!*' he whines.

'Try to understand, Pranav. They not only insulted me but also accused me of things that I hadn't done. If I go back, it will mean that I have accepted that they were right and I was wrong.'

'I do not understand what you are saying at all, sir-ji! How does this mean that you were wrong? That sexy potato has made you an offer. That means *he* is apologizing for what he did!'

I look back at him thoughtfully.

'He is giving in, sir-ji. Please don't be so stiff.'

Silence.

'Sir-ji, you are being very selfish. Do you even know how much pain we've suffered and how much effort we have put into this? How much we had to fight to get you back? You cannot do this, sir-ji, you have to come back. We *need* you, sir-ji!'

With a dramatic smile, I say, 'You do not need me, you want me back.'

'Oh please, sir-ji! Please don't start with your filmy philosophy again,' he cuts me off and I become quiet.

Maybe he is right. I look at him and start thinking about it. He wants me back . . . he really, really wants me back. I can see it in his eyes—he is almost desperate. And maybe he is right, maybe I am thinking only about myself right now. Maybe my going back will help the kids.

'And you need this job, sir-ji. What do you think—that I don't know anything? I know everything, sir-ji. I have heard you and Nisha ma'am talk so many times in the night about how you need to get a job and how you are running out of money. It's a small house, sir-ji, and the walls are thin. You have to take this job, sir-ji!'

Oh my God! He has been listening to everything we have been saying and doing in our room! Oh my God!

7

Writing is not an easy business—Jeet

It's been a crazy day at our office today. We have been going mad with all the meetings we've attended since morning. Three events have to be organized and co-ordinated for the PR activity. There were so many things scheduled for today that we are still stuck here, even though it's nearly eight. Neeti is still in front of the computer organizing the '*PR and promotions*' folder—scans of all the reviews and articles that appeared in newspapers and magazines, and links to online stories of the media coverage and audio clips of our radio interviews.

I glance around our office and everything looks just right—everything is in complete order, from my office table to each and every file on the shelves. At times I find it hard to believe that I have achieved all this.

'Sharma from the Red Store called again today. He wants more discounts he said, he wants us to help him negotiate with the publisher.'

'Did you tell him further discounts aren't possible? Our

publisher is already giving him books on a 60 per cent discount. What—he wants the books for free? Revert with a firm no.'

'Of course I told him that. What do you think I am? Foolish?'

'What did he say?'

'He did not agree. He said that there are far too many books in the market these days; over three hundred books are published every month. If we want more visibility for our books, we should give him more discounts.'

'This Sharma is really giving us a lot of problems. I've heard he hasn't even cleared his last payment.'

'That's true. Moron! I really don't have the mental strength to deal with idiots like him.' Neeti sounds cross.

'Hey, what's wrong? Why so irritated today?'

Neeti is not like this as a rule. In fact, she is the one who usually deals with the public and handles these people.

She turns around and gives me a very irritated look, 'Why do all these articles have to talk as if it's only you who does all the work, as if it's only you who does all the writing? They make it sound like I do nothing. When in reality I am the one doing all the writing and you're the one writing *nothing*.'

'Because anyone can write but not everyone can sell it,' I joke.

'What do you mean?' She looks furious now.

Okay, I need to temper what I just said. This is no time to mention the fact that our books sell only on the strength of my name. 'We both know there are so many books in the market better than what we write but our books sell more than those.'

'What does that mean? What does that have to do with what I just said? It makes no sense.'

'Why do you always have to find sense in everything?'

She just looks back at me with the same expression.

'You know what one of my fantasies have always been?' I continue.

'Shut up.'

'Doing it here . . . on the office table.' I get up and walk towards her. 'Just swipe everything off the table and have mad, wild S-E-X!'

I hold her by the shoulders and kiss her on the neck and softly nip her earlobes. She does not move away, she does not resist. I slide my hands under her thighs and pick her up from her chair. She wraps her legs around my waist. I walk up to the table, put her on it, swipe the table clean in one single, smooth move. I unbutton her crisp white shirt and push it off her smooth round shoulders. I slide my hand up her back and unhook her bra, revealing her firm round breasts. She makes a move, holds my lower lip between her teeth, bites it hard and pulls it even harder. It's hurting but I like this pain. I cup her breasts; her nipples are hard. She bites my lip even harder and pulls it again. I hold her by her waist and press her pelvis against mine. She grabs on to my shoulder firmly, digs her nails into my skin and runs them across my chest. The long red welts burn with pain. She smiles cruelly, grabs me by my shoulders, pushes me around to switch our positions, stares at me with burning desire in her eyes and pushes me away. My back hits the table. She unbuttons my jeans, pulls them down and pounces on me.

8

Some people really believe any publicity is good publicity—Karun

He still has the fire burning inside him; I know it only needs to be fanned a little. But this guy, D.K. Dé, is something, I have to admit. After that One-Day-Lit-Fest-of-the-Year episode, even I felt for a while that his days in publishing were over. Whereas instead of going out of business, this guy worked hard and *expanded* his publishing house even more. '*Any publicity is good publicity*,' he always says and he turned the whole controversy that had blown up against him to his own advantage. He had a whole ad campaign on Facebook compelling people to 'read the books from the publisher who won't pay his authors' after creating a fake profile with a random name that had a sleazy picture of a half-naked girl. Everyone wanted to read the books of those poor authors and here we are—in an office occupying two full floors in a new building. He even has a senior editor now who has slightly quirky mannerisms and seems like his playmate but then, what do I care? He can fuck anyone he wants as long as he stays away from me.

I am sitting in his office, waiting for him to finish his work and talk to me. I would have preferred to wait in the reception but he insisted I wait inside, and made me sit on the chair right in front of him.

'So, Karun, tell me. How have you been?' he asks, pressing a final key on the keyboard and turning to me.

'Good, sir, how are you?'

'Good. You look very fit. Are you going to the gym these days?' He is checking me out.

'Actually, yes.'

'This is the best age to start exercising. Your hormones are just at the right levels at this age. You will get results very fast.'

'I hope so, sir.'

'Let me see,' he reaches forward and feels my bicep and pecs. 'Hmm, I see results.'

'Thank you.' I smile. Feel me all you want. Just publish my books and sell them, give me larger print runs. 'Sir, I was just thinking, what Rohit did to you at that lit fest is not done. He humiliated you publicly, sir, and he had no right to do that. You made him what he is and that is how he repaid you? He should pay for it, sir. You should make him pay for all the humiliation and false accusations he hurled at you. Why would you ever cheat any author out of his royalties? What would you get out of it?'

Dé is looking at me in silence; I meet his gaze patiently.

'He humiliated *me*, he accused *me*. Why does it bother *you* so much?' he finally speaks.

'Because unlike him, I appreciate what you have done for

me, sir. You are the one who believed in my work when no one else did and made me what I am today.'

He is still looking at me. He is not convinced. I have to sweeten the pot somehow, make him trust me. 'And because he humiliated me as well. He threw eggs and tomatoes at me in front of everyone, in public. He had no reason to do that. He is a mad man, sir, and he needs to be taught a lesson.'

'Don't worry. He will pay his dues. He will pay for what he has done,' D.K. Dé smiles.

9

What is a celebrity without a 'leaked' sex tape—Jeet

Readers love me. And it feels really great to know that. The Lucknow launch of our book was today and after the event, I had to sit for a good hour or so to sign all the books they wanted me to sign.

'Quite a crowd we had today!' I say to Neeti back in the hotel room. She has just come out of the bathroom after a shower and is drying her black wavy hair, spraying tiny drops of water around.

She does not look at me. 'It's really funny how you hog all the attention all the time. I was only asked to sign a total of ten books today.'

'Because I am the *star*. That was the reason why you followed and met me in the first place, remember?'

She continues fluffing her hair with the towel and ignoring me. Clearly, she is not happy about what I just said.

I change the topic.

'Aanush was suggesting that we should generate a

controversy. It will help the sales of our books.'

'Hmm.'

'I was thinking maybe we can create some kind of controversy revolving around Mr De. For cheating me. He should pay for that in some way.'

'Oh please, Jeet. No one is interested in a middle-aged pervert hitting on his under-age male authors. Besides, this whole thing was already done to death last year after the One-Day-Lit-Fest-of-the-Year, remember?'

She is right. We need to come up with something else. I try to find another way to create a controversy but I find myself distracted by Neeti. She is not wearing a bra and her firm, round breasts are shaping the thin grey cotton T-shirt she is wearing to bed. She looks so sexy! I bite my lip and try to think.

'You know something? Maybe we can just leak a sex video of us on the Internet. How does that sound?'

This is a brilliant idea—I know that.

Neeti squints and looks at me, 'Hmm . . . tell me more.'

'We videotape ourselves having some really great, hot sex and then just put the video on the Internet! *Everyone* will watch it. After all, everyone watches sex videos and porn. Even people who say they don't watch sex videos, watch them. Of course, we will fix the frame of the video so that our faces are not visible. This will just make us so outrageously popular!'

She looks like she's thinking about it and, after a few minutes, says, 'This may work actually.'

'It's going to more than work, Neeti. This is the best idea we could have ever thought of.' I pull my iPad out of my bag and set it on the table. I set the camera to record and fix the frame.

'Come on now, let's do it.' I quickly take my shirt off. I am already hard just thinking about all this.

She stares at my well-toned body. 'You know you have one of the best bodies I have seen.'

'Yes, and why do you think I work on that?' I say as I unbutton my jeans and step out of them.

She smiles and slowly takes off her T-shirt. I love what I see. I pull her into my arms and run my hand up her side. Oh! The touch of her smooth, tight, supple skin! Her body is made for sex! I run my finger around her nipple and lick her collarbone. She runs her hand down my chest to between my legs. Oh this pleasure! I hug her tight and we both fall on the bed. I kiss her breasts and say, 'Please be a little gentle this time. Last time when we did it on the office table, you almost used sex as a weapon. I was sore for days after that.'

She bites my lower lip, pulls at it, gives me a look filled with lust, 'Then don't say anything to piss me off this time . . .'

10

**Yes, he joined back, but he was really left with no
other choice—Rohit**

He looks the same. He is still as fat and ugly as ever. His
office has changed a bit though. It looks a bit cleaner and
things are kept in a more orderly fashion. I've walked into
Gurinder Singh's office and a major difference that I see is
that Jabba is not reading an erotic book and his hands are
not in an inappropriate place. Good! Now I won't need to
turn my eyes away and pretend I haven't seen anything and
sing a song in my head to seem all casual and breezy and not
terribly uncomfortable. He is going through some papers and
is signing some documents without even reading them. After
a few seconds, he is finished with the pile of documents and
pushes them aside.

'So, Rohit, how's everything? How is your writing going?'

'It's going good, sir. I am working on my third book.'

'Did you settle your dispute with your publisher? It was
quite a bold move I must say.'

I smile. So he has been keeping track of me.

'Not really, sir. The whole thing was a hot piece of gossip for people for a while and then things just fizzled out.'

He smiles and says, 'That is what always happens. Standing up and unmasking people does not really work in today's world. You should have been smarter and dealt with him differently.'

I wonder what he means. What other way could there have been to deal with the situation? He looks at me and I know he senses the questions running in my mind but he does not give me any answers. The door opens and a young girl in her early twenties enters the room. She is wearing a dark-blue fitted T-shirt with black trousers that are totally accentuating her attractive figure.

'Good morning, sir.' She nods and greets Jabba as if she is some soldier reporting to her boss.

'Morning,' Jabba utters.

The girl comes and stands by my side as if waiting for orders. Jabba speaks up, 'Rohit, this is Megha. She has graduated from this college and will be joining here as faculty now. She is a brilliant teacher. In fact I would say that she is the best teacher we have got, the *best*.' He closes his eyes tightly, emphasizing the word 'best' to make his point.

'Hello,' I turn and greet her as she nods and greets me back.

'Megha and you will be teaching the final year students together. Both of you will conduct the graphics and painting studio.'

'Cool.' It will be nice to have co-faculty for the studio. Things will be easier to manage.

'I don't know what kind of magic you cast on the students,

Rohit, but they made my life miserable to get you back,' Jabba says.

I just smile at him awkwardly. I really don't know what to say.

He sighs loudly. 'All right then, the classes will start on Monday. You can take a copy of the syllabus from the HOD,' he says, shooting me a look. 'You can prepare for the studio over the weekend.'

'Cool.'

There is a moment of silence and I decide to leave.

'Okay, sir, see you on Monday.'

'Okay, Rohit.'

His behaviour is completely different from what I have seen in the past.

'Sit, Megha, I want to discuss a few things . . .' he says as I walk out of his office.

School and college buildings are funny in ways. Most of them are old and outdated and remain practically unchanged over decades even though most of the people in these buildings change practically every year.

I am walking in the same corridors I used to march up and down in every day when, worked here earlier. I see students standing and sitting in the same spots as they did back then. The students have changed; there are new faces but the expressions, gestures and feelings they exhibit are the same. So much drama has happened so many times in this very corridor. This was where I was once outrageously humiliated by Jabba when he said that my books are only good enough to be read while sitting on the toilet as it's best to read them and flush them in a single go! But he seems to have changed now, and for the better. He did not make any derogatory remarks today.

As I walk into the faculty room I am bombarded with memories. I walk to the HOD's cabin and stand in the doorway, waiting for her to be free. She is squinting and frowning and staring into her laptop when she notices me.

'Rohit, come, sit!'

'Hello, ma'am, how are you?' I sit down.

'Things are all right. Not the best but . . . it's okay. Tell me, how have you been?'

'Things have been good, ma'am. It kind of feels good to be back.' I smile.

She looks at me as if I am an innocent lamb who is bleating happily and has no idea of what is happening around it.

'Things have changed a bit in the past few months. The dean has made a lot of changes and not all of them for the best.'

'Really? What kind of changes?' I am curious.

'Right now is not the best time to talk about it,' she says as she turns back to her laptop screen and resumes typing.

'The dean asked me to take the syllabus from you.'

'Yes, I am just giving a printout,' she says as a printed A4 sheet of paper starts to roll out of the printer on her table. 'You have been allotted the final year art studio.'

'Yes, ma'am.'

'And you will be teaching with Megha. She will be your co-faculty.'

'Yes, she seemed nice.'

'So you have met her already?'

'Yeah, I just met her in the dean's office.'

She has a strange look in her eyes as if she has something on her mind but she is holding it back.

'Why . . . why are you looking at me like that?' I ask. 'Is there something I should keep in mind while working with her?'

'No . . . nothing, really. It's the final year students whom you will be handling this year. Their thesis projects, which is the most important part of their portfolios when they start their careers as professionals, will begin soon,' she says and then smiles faintly. 'I am happy you are here; I think you are the best person for the job. It's nice to have you with us again, Rohit, welcome back!'

We shake hands.

It feels nice to be back.

11

You can make yourself famous, you can destroy others: you can do it all if you have money—Karun

They say that the media has been sold and it's something to worry about. I think that is just flying horse shit. It's nothing to worry about; it's a *good* thing. I mean, finally, we have come to a system with which we can reach a huge number of people and say what we want to say. They provide us a service and we pay them for it. And it all makes sense. Take a simple thing: a newspaper review, for example. There are so many books being written these days. It's almost impossible for any newspaper or magazine to review all of them. So they review only the ones that pay them, otherwise how can they ever choose? And it doesn't even cost that much. I am at Starbucks to meet journalist Vishal Singh. These days everyone is on Facebook, which is where I got in touch with him. It wasn't difficult to strike a deal.

He opens the door and enters the café. I look at my watch—5 p.m. He's right on time. Perfect! I like people who are punctual.

'Hey!' I get up and shake hands with him.

'Hi,' he says as he puts his black bag on the floor next to the chair and sits down.

'What would you like to have?' I ask.

'Caramel macchiato,' he says. Some expensive taste he has. I go to the counter, place the order and come back.

'So tell me, Karun, how do you want me to proceed?' he demands once I've sat down.

'The basic idea is to get my book reviewed.'

'Okay,' he nods.

'And since we are having an *understanding*, I am assuming that it will be a positive review.'

'Fair enough.'

'Cool.' I smile

'Okay. So let's settle the finances.'

'Yes.'

'As we discussed earlier, it will cost seven grand.' He states the figure as if it's the fixed MRP of a product.

'Come on, man! You've got to give me a discount! I am only a student, I don't even have a job!'

He only smiles and looks back at me. Okay, I get the point: he is going write a review, people will read it and buy my book and I will make money out of it.

I beg for a discount again. 'After all, I have given you so many secrets about Mr De.'

He only smiles and looks back at me again. Clearly, my request is not having any effect on him.

'Okay. Five thousand and we have a deal.' I pull out five thousand-rupee notes and put them on the table in front of him. He does not even touch them, only sits back in his chair calmly.

'Fine! Seven it is. But then you have to do one more little thing for me,' I say as I take out two crisp thousand-rupee notes and put them on the table like I'm an actor in a movie about poker players.

Vishal looks back at me with questioning eyes.

'You have to write some despicably bad stuff about Rohit Sehdev.'

He leans forward, picks up the money and says, 'And can I ask why you want me to do this "one more little thing"?'

'It's a long story. I'll tell you some other time.'

Just then the lady behind the counter calls out 'Karun!'

'I guess our coffee is ready!'

Perfect.

12

**It's really sad how at times we want to help someone
out of their misery but can't as we are so busy with
our own lives—Rohit**

It's happening! It's finally reaching somewhere. I think I have
got my story on track now. I just need a few more months and
I think I will be done with the manuscript. And this is going
to create history! It's going to be the hottest-selling book in
years. And controversial—*are the incidents in the book real? The
things it says about Vikram Rawat—are they all true?* People
are going to ask questions left, right and centre once copies
hit the market. I am planning to write around fifty thousand
words, which should make it a novel of around two hundred
and fifty pages or so—an easy read, neither long, nor short.
The feeling of finally seeing a fulfilling result of my struggle
and effort makes me so excited that I am hungry. I want to eat
something right now so I go to the kitchen to make myself a
salami sandwich with mayonnaise. Just then the doorbell rings.
I look at my wrist watch. It's 8 p.m. This has to be Nisha; she

must be back from office. I open the door; she walks in and puts her bag on the side table.

'I am going to make sandwiches. Would you like to have some?'

'No, not right now . . .' She sounds tired.

I walk to the kitchen and she follows me and stands next to me as I take a slice of brown whole-grain bread and spread the mayonnaise on it. She puts her arms around me. I take her hand and gently kiss it. She is definitely upset about something. She only makes warm physical contact if she's feeling very romantic or she is upset. And looking at her right now, I can bet she is not feeling romantic.

'What happened?' I ask concerned.

'Nothing,' she sighs deeply.

'Come on! Tell me,' I squeeze her hand lightly.

She leans her head against my back and takes another deep breath, 'You remember my journalist friend, Meetali?'

'Of course I do. The one who agreed to review my last book and got mad at me when we were not able to send her a copy.'

'Yeah. She is not mad at you any more by the way,' she says as she walks back to the room. 'Her cousin, Tara, lost her boyfriend recently. It's really very tragic. They had been together since childhood. I just met her today. She is really miserable. I just sat there in silence, looking at her as she kept sobbing. I wanted to help her, to make her feel better. But I couldn't do anything. I felt so . . . helpless. Such couples are rare, Rohit, people don't love each other like that these days . . .'

'God! I am so sorry to hear that. But what happened to him?'

'It was a drug overdose. It really worries me the way our generation is heading. Such a fine life, and ended in such a terrible manner that could have been avoided.'

'That is really terrible,' I shake my head. This sounds awful. I think of the girl, her love for the guy and then think about our love. What if something were to happen to one of us? How would we survive? And my heart begins to explode.

'In fact, he was a student in the same college where you teach. He was perusing his masters' degree in fine arts I think.'

'Oh,' I don't know what to say. I have seen this menace of drugs in the college but never encountered such devastating consequences.

'God, it feels terrible when I think about it . . .' she shakes her head.

I give her a tight hug and we stand there, in each other's arms, drawing comfort from the fact that we are together. It feels like we will never move away and I'm perfectly happy to stay here like this.

Then Nisha pulls away. She wipes the tears from her eyes and fixes her hair. I give her a protective kiss.

'Are we not going to the party?' she asks

I look at her blankly. 'What party?'

'Have you forgotten?' she asks frowning.

I had been so busy and engrossed in my writing that I really had forgotten.

It's a big party that a national newspaper is throwing here in Delhi. It's supposed to be this huge, cultural event in the city where the who's who of today's art and culture world will be in attendance—celebrity artists, sculptors, filmmakers, authors, fashion designers—everyone. It's going to be *the* place to make contacts.

Who knows, I might even meet a famous author whom I will become wonderful friends with over a couple of drinks and get a quote for my next novel. Or maybe a very well-known celebrity would like to write a quote—that will help too. That's how world works, that's how everything functions.

'It's an important party. You don't know who you might meet there. Networking is essential these days. That is the only way to advance one's career,' she says as she walks to the bathroom.

'I am going be ready in ten minutes!' I shout to make sure that she can hear me in the bathroom.

'Where is Pranav by the way? Isn't he supposed to be home right now?' Nisha comes out of the bathroom tying her hair in a bun. She has splashed her face with water to wash off the fatigue and looks so fresh. She should never wear any make-up.

'Friend's place. Group assignment.' I shrug.

'I think you need to supervise his actions. He may be up to no good.' Nisha walks back into the bathroom.

I know I should but for some reason all I can think about is Nisha.

13

Underneath it all—sex, lies and videotapes—Jeet

CRAZY HOT SEX VIDEO GONE VIRAL!

And now we know what lies underneath their clothes and the way they like to do it. A sex video of Jeet and Neeti has 'somehow' leaked on the Internet and from what is being observed, it has left people asking for more as the video ends just when things are getting hot! Reading the comments on the video, one cannot miss the fact that people are going crazy about the 'hot bodies' of the two sexy authors. The myth that authors are 'geeky' people with fat and sloppy bodies has been busted. Writers are the new sexy!

It's another happy morning in the cosy little set-up we call office. The sex tape is out and the media is talking about it just the way we wanted them to.

'We got it right this time again!' I laugh and look at Neeti who is working at her station right now.

'Yeah,' she replies flatly.

'What's wrong with you? Come on! You should be happy about it! We are back in the news!'

She turns her chair around and looks at me, 'Jeet, we are authors, not whores who need to show their bodies to people to make them realize our worth.'

'Oh come on! Now don't go all "Sati-Savitri" on me. No one forced you into doing anything. Cheer up! This is *good*!'

She stares at me for a few seconds and then shrugs, 'Of course, how will you ever understand. It's I who do all the writing. I am the writer in our team!'

'Hey, hey, hey! What's up with you today? Yes, you do write more than I do but you cannot deny that the books sell on my name. You've been working with me long enough to know it's not easy to sell books. Any idiot can write a book; but only a genius can sell his books.'

She turns to her computer and starts working again. I don't like her attitude. She needs to be tamed. She is flying too high in the sky right now, unaware of the realities of the publishing business. It's impossible to sell a book without creating a buzz in the media. If we do not catch the attention the way we are doing then we are only going to get buried under the tall piles of our books. The stress here is making me go crazy and all she can think of is authors should not have to shed their *clothes*? This is not something I want to spend my time thinking about; I have way more important things to focus on right now.

As I quickly scan the other stories in the newspaper, I notice the headline of an article at the bottom corner of the last page.

WRITING FOR LOVE AND FOR THE LOVE OF WRITING

Karun Mukharjee is not even out of his teens yet and has already become one of the most celebrated authors of Indian romance fiction. His new book, *My Love, My Angel is the Best Thing in My Life*, is the hottest-selling title in bookstores across the country. When asked what he has to say about his book, the author smiled and said, 'I only—

'Jeet, something is wrong. I think we need to look into this,' Neeti interrupts me.

I put the paper down and turn to her. 'What is it?'

'This has been going on for a while but things have become crazy suddenly,' she says as I look at the computer screen in front of her. 'Every now and then we've been getting these hate mails and bad reviews that make a lot of personal comments but now they are just flooding in,' she continues.

I scroll down the list and there are quite a few. One of the reviews reads:

The book was so pathetic that I had to roll my eyes at every line printed. Thanks to Jeet and Neeti now I can even see out of the back of my head. Their book is priced at 200 rupees but I will not even pay two sorry dimes for it.

'This is insane.'

'Something is fishy, I think,' Neeti mutters without looking at me.

'I'll look into it.'

'Do it later. For now I think we should leave or we'll be late for the party.'

'Oh God! I completely forgot! The Grand Gatsby Party! Damn! I can't come.'

'Why?' Neeti asks, rising from the chair.

'I have to go for this dinner meeting with the CEO of the Red Book Store chain of bookshops and his wife. I'm hoping to crack a good deal with them. If they place a bulk order for our new book, it will help us a lot.'

'It would be great if that happens,' Neeti says as she turns off the computer. 'Though it would have been nice if you had come to the party. The who's who of the publishing industry is going to be there. It will be a great contact-building exercise.'

'Well, you can be the face of our writing team today then. Tap the contacts.' I smile.

'Yes, I will do that. See you tomorrow!' she says and walks out of the room.

I turn around and look at the blank screen of the computer. Those were some terrible mails. They did not seem genuine to me though; they read like the rantings of a fucking unprofessional reviewer. Something is wrong. I need to get to the bottom of this.

14

She feels she has lost everything but she will live on to keep the love that she has lost alive, she will live on—Tara

She has a whole almirah-full of the gifts Tarun had given her over the years. She looks at the pile of T-shirts he had given her. It was a ritual of sorts for them—they would gift each other a T-shirt once every month with a special thought printed on it for the other person, many times with a picture of the two of them. There is a whole bunch of other things like key chains, cute toys and photo frames inside the almirah. She stares at the gifts blankly. She had put them inside because she couldn't bear to look at them when they were kept around the room. Now when she looks at them, she is numb. She is not living in the present. Right now she can only remember the time when Tarun proposed to her. They were in the fifth standard back then; it seems silly when she thinks of it now. Then they were only good friends who shared all their secrets with each other, told each other every detail of what was going on in their lives. They even took turns to do each other's homework. They cried together when Tarun's dog Ruffle died. They had sat next to Ruffle's grave for hours holding each other's hands, Tarun with his head on Tara's shoulder. They were teenagers then. They had never imagined life without each other. And now Tarun is dead. Tara is still trying to understand this fact. She has lost all sense of time. Morning, evening, afternoon, day or night—it all feels the same to her.

She gets up and closes her almirah.

'Tara, beta, please come for breakfast,' her mother calls for the tenth time now. Breathing, eating and sleeping have become a mechanical process for her now. Like a robot, she goes to the dining room. Her mother serves her scrambled eggs, orange juice and toasts with apple jam. This used to be her favourite breakfast but now these are only things she needs to chew and swallow to keep herself from starving—they do not make her feel any better. Actually, nothing makes her feel better. She is in a constant state of restlessness and agony. Like someone is ripping her heart out and shredding it into pieces and repeating the whole process again as soon as it is over. She is in hell, unable to breathe.

She starts to gobble her breakfast when her mother sits down next to her.

'You should go to college today,' she says, putting her hand on Tara's shoulder.

Tara shakes her head and immediately her eyes are wet.

Her mother hugs her, 'Beta, you must be strong. Tarun would never want you to be in this state.'

Tara lets out a little laugh as her eyes well up. 'You think you understand what Tarun would want? You think you understand what I am feeling? You understand nothing. You have no idea what it feels like to have lost the one you love the most. But I do. I know what it feels like to lose the love of your life. And I understand why some people might want to kill themselves—why they want to commit suicide. It is because they are catapulted into a state of constant misery that cannot be brought to an end by any means. The feeling is like an insect that eats you from the inside and makes you hollow, leaving only your heart to flutter in that cavity. You begin to believe that nothing in this world at all can improve your state. But you desperately want to end this state; you desperately want to get out of it. And the only thing that can erase the pain and emptiness is death; you come to believe that you can end what you are feeling only if you end your life. And so you kill yourself. I understand this because I feel this way.'

Tara's mother has a big lump in her throat. She has to take care of her daughter even more now. She cannot leave her alone for even a single minute. She does not want Tara to do something as stupid as commit suicide. But she does not interrupt her. For this is the first time Tara is pouring her heart out after Tarun's death. She wants her to vent her feelings.

Tara looks at her mother and notices the panic in her eyes. She lets out a little laugh and says, 'But don't worry. I am not going kill myself. I will never do something that stupid. Tarun may be dead for the whole world but he is still alive with me. No one can take away from me the times we spent together, the memories I have. I will live, for he lives inside me, he lives in my heart. And I will never let him die.'

15

He has always believed that if you can't win it over, kill it—Karun

This is a large party and I like large parties. And top it all, it's a Gatsby-themed party—the epitome of glamour and success. Such parties are a gateway to fame and riches. I have come here to do what every young, emerging author must do at a party like this—give a copy of your book to all the celebrities present, grab them by the shoulder, get a picture taken with them while they're holding your book and share it on Facebook. This gets you the kind of popularity one can't even imagine. Everyone from Vikram Rawat to that pathetic, miserable loser Rohit Sehdev is here. There is a huge crowd of journalists hounding Vikram like a pack of wolves surrounding their prey. There are microphones with big black blow-cutters in many hands and cameras are flashing around him like lightning in a thunderstorm. He has a permanent smile plastered on his face, though he seems a bit preoccupied right now. I can't pierce the crowd mobbing him so I'll get the job done later.

But before that I have something more important to do. I am walking towards my aim when I notice someone whom I need to speak to. I am going to have a quick 'talk' and then get the picture I need.

Neeti, Jeet's writing partner and sex buddy, is walking towards me. But she does not recognize me. Of course, we've never met. I need to get rolling with my plan.

'Hello, ma'am,' I walk up to her.

She is a little baffled to suddenly see me in front of her but still manages a smile.

'Hi,' she responds, giving me a do-I-know-you? look.

'My name is Karun. I am an author. I would like to present my debut novel to you.' I take a copy of my novel from my bag and hand it to her. 'And I would love for you to give me your valuable comments on it.'

'Sure,' she smiles, 'thank you'.

'I must say I am a huge fan of your work. So many books written in such a short span of time . . . hats off, ma'am, hats off.'

'Thank you.' She looks at the book in her hands, 'Karun Mukharjee, I have heard about you.'

'Really? What?'

'I think I read about you in the newspapers.'

'Okay,' I smile. So people are reading those articles. *Nice!*

There are a few seconds of awkward silence and then I speak up, 'Ma'am, if you have a few minutes, I would like to talk to you about something.'

'Sure, go ahead.'

'I have a story in mind that I want to co-author with you.'

My declaration is followed by silence. She is looking at me without saying anything; it's as if she wants me to continue.

'It's the story of an accidental author who gets his hands on someone else's manuscript and has it published under his own name. The book becomes a huge bestseller and the author becomes a huge hit. He has an infinite hunger for fame that can never be fulfilled. It will be a story of his journey through life.'

Silence.

She is lost in thought, probably thinking the story has all the masala we need for a story. Or she is baffled by how I know all these secrets. She has no idea of my abilities, my contacts.

'What do you think?' I nudge.

'It's interesting, I'll think about it.'

'Thank you! Thank you so much!' I shake hands with her to show my excitement. 'You are the best!' This is it! Half the battle is won now. Splitting Jeet and Neeti is going to be a piece of cake. These people have no idea whom they are dealing with! I am going to destroy them all!

16

Big parties can actually kill some people
—Rohit

'A little party never killed no body. I am gonna dance until I drop . . .'

Loud music blares from the mammoth speakers as we walk into this magnificent party on the open lawn. It's a Gatsby-themed party and the scale and glamour of the décor is mind-blowing.

So many famous people are here and yet there is no one I actually know. But it's okay; I'll just sit in a corner like an invisible person, a nobody.

Nisha holds my hand and gives it a soft squeeze. 'Please, there is no point being so grumpy. Move around! Mingle with the other guests!'

'Okay, fine!' she says, exasperated with my silence. 'Let's go and sit at that table,' she points to an empty table that has a tall arrangement of different coloured gladioli in the centre.

I continuously drum my fingers on the table after we've

sat down, looking for a waiter from whose tray I can snatch something to eat to keep myself momentarily busy, although that will only make me fat! *Why do I come to parties?* Why do I have such a terrible memory that I forget the last traumatizing party experience? 'Little party never killed nobody,' they say. Yeah, right.

'Oh my God!' Nisha suddenly jumps. 'That is Virath Seth!'

'Wow! That is so cool! Er . . . who is he?'

'Oh come on! You don't know Virath Seth? He is *the* most expensive sculpture artist of our time. His last piece was sold for a mind-boggling 1.2 million dollars!'

'Really?'

'I knew he was in India but I didn't know he would be here, at this party!'

'Oh, okay.'

'God! I must go and meet him. I'll be back in a while.'

'Sure.'

She hurriedly gets up and leaves while I look around at people's faces in the party without any reason or purpose. What else is one supposed to do at a party where you do not know anyone? It's seriously beyond me to understand how people can be so happy at a party. I mean, just look around! Women in shiny dresses and holding wine glasses are throwing their heads back and laughing as they listen to the men hovering around them, constantly staring at their cleavages like hungry wolves. It's simply disgusting.

Most of the men at the party are wearing suits. God! I am not even appropriately dressed for the occasion! I mean who comes to a party like this in a plain white shirt and blue jeans? I keep looking at the people around me when, suddenly, I realize that I know one of them. It's Karun Mukharjee. Oh God! I do not want to talk to him! I am about to look away and pretend that I haven't seen him when Karun turns his head and spots me. He waves at me but I ignore him and look the other way.

In less than fifteen seconds he is standing in front of me.

'Hey!' he says.

'Hi! How are you? Didn't know you were here too.'

'Oh come on, I saw that look of shock when you saw me and then looked away.'

I look back at him, dumbstruck.

'It's okay.' He sits down.

What the hell is wrong with him? Why is he sitting down? Does he not know I hate his guts? He has to go away!

'So, how are you? What are you doing these days?'

'I am working on my next book.' I really do not want to talk to him.

'Is that so?'

'Yes. Why would you ask that?' I want to punch him in the face.

'Nothing just . . . I was thinking that since your last book was such a disaster and didn't sell at *all*, you might be thinking of shifting your focus from writing to something that you are actually good at.' He looks down at the table, starts shaking his head and laughs, 'You know something? When I met you for the first time, I kind of believed that you were actually a good contender for the Popular Book Awards. But now just look at you . . . the whole thing actually sounds like a joke.'

I want to grab him by his neck and rip his head off but I

look away and do not say anything.

'I also heard that you were fired from your post at that college and that you are jobless now?' His eyes are fixed on me, like a hawk's.

'They did not fire me, I resigned—'

He cuts me off. 'Yeah, yeah. That is what one says wh—'

'And I joined back, by the way,' I retort, happily cutting him off in turn.

He looks at me with his mouth open.

'You know something, Karun . . .' I say, 'you are never going make it as a writer—'

But he cuts me off again! 'Look at you. Lying at the bottom of the pit after your huge failure, yet still so positive and preachy! You really amaze me. You know what happened, right?'

I look back at him, confused. Does he know something about me that I don't?

'You know why your last book flopped, right?'

'What do you mean?'

'Oh come on! Don't tell me that you don't know. Your publisher killed your book because of the humiliation you caused him. And if you ask me, I don't really blame him. What was he supposed to do after you treated him the way you did in public? He wants to end your career as a writer and he will. He is never going to let you out of your contract. You are doomed. Even the gods would pity you right now.'

What he is telling me is only obvious. But I know that hard work can change anything. I just need to get a good book out next and that will change everything. This time I will have the support of a better publisher too.

'You know something? Actually I pity you, Karun, because you are a corrupt person with an ugly heart. And writing stories is an art that is meaningful only if it touches the readers' hearts. And an ugly heart can never produce anything beautiful enough to touch someone's heart. It's *you* who are wasting your time, not me. You should give up writing and study engineering or get an MBA or something,' I respond angrily.

'Just listen to you.' Karun squints. 'What you are saying, or rather what you believe is *wrong*. I am really sorry for being the one to break this to you but the truth is that . . . you see, you were, or rather *are* unsuccessful in making a living from your writing. You were not really able to follow your heart and your dreams and live the way you wanted to. And that is why you are saying this—because you want to convince yourself and want others to fail, only because *you* failed.' He shakes his head. 'You want everyone's life and career to be as miserable as yours. Tch . . . tch . . . tch . . .' He clicks his tongue. 'You say you pity me? I pity you more!'

'What you are saying is not true,' I retort sharply. 'I don't want bad things to happen to others. It's you who want that, not me!'

He is a miserable person. He's is so blind and drunk on his success, it's not even funny. His actions will have terrible consequences. He has no right to say the things he has said but it's okay. He is very young and has so much to learn. I just need to ignore him and make sure to stay away from him in the future.

He squints and gives me a dirty look. 'Are you accusing me of something?'

'I am not accusing you of anything. It's only your guilt that is making you feel so.'

'You know something, I just wish that you hadn't said what you did, because they say that words are wind . . . but you never know what impact that wind might have on your life.' He gives me a hard look, gets up and leaves.

I'm feeling quite sick as I watch him walk away.

17

When these new books catch the attention of the king of Hindi cinema—Ravi Kapoor

His limbs are rendered weak but his mind and heart still pump with vigour and energy; it is evident in the way he walks, sits and speaks. He is fifteen minutes early for the meeting; just like he has been for each and every meeting he has conducted or attended in the last fifty years. Filmmaking is the passion of passions for him—there are not many things in the world that give him as much pleasure. Sitting at the head of the twenty-four-seater table, he drums his fingers and looks around the board room that has posters of all the films he has made in his half-a-century-long career. 'Fifty years!' he thinks. 'Fifty years is not a short span of time.' It has been an age, an era during which he has ruled the film industry.

Much has changed over the years—cinematography, music, visuals and other elements have all grown and metamorphosed. Even the patterns of filmmaking and the structures of narrations have changed and evolved over the decades. He has discovered many actors; made them superstars who ruled the screens all over the nation for a time and then slowly faded away. But he has persevered, for he has adapted. Having directed his first film at the age of twenty-seven, he has been working tirelessly ever since.

His eyes travel from one corner of the boardroom to the other, looking at all the film posters. He has made films, he has made blockbusters. Some of them created nationwide movements. Others were failures. But he has stayed. It has not been easy to build this huge empire. He has sacrificed a lot; he has given up the possibilities of life and relationships to achieve all that he has today.

The board members and the rest of the team enter the board room one by one, none of them late for the meeting.

It is a rule that only he shall open the meetings. He has been choosing in his mind the words he wants to say for a while now.

'The problem with a lot of filmmakers today is that they have lost faith in new stories. No one is writing with honesty these days. Everyone wants to play it safe. No one cares to tell a story; they only want to make sure if it will *work* or not. They don't understand that if a story is not written with honesty, it will never work. And this is the reason we have so many films being remade or copied from Hollywood. But I have not lost faith. I still believe that there are some people out there who do write with honesty. I want to find one such story and make a film with it. It will be the biggest film of my career. And I know it will work. Because for that film, all of you and I will work with full honesty. My son is coming back from Prague after completing his master's degree in cinema and digital media. I want to find a new story before he arrives. There are a lot of young authors these days who are writing wonderful, honest, very honest novels. I want you all to shortlist five such novels and bring them to me.'

With that the agenda for the meeting has been set. There is going to be a hunt, a contest to seek out new talent.

Ravi Kapoor smiles with satisfaction. It is good to think of new and exciting things to do. His work is paramount but it could not have been so had he not looked at greener pastures and fresh talent throughout his career. It is this freedom to do what he enjoys the most in his life which he cherishes, for there is no greater joy in the world than that—do what you love to do, for as long as you live.

18

He thinks that he is singing the best duet with Megha then goes ahead and dances with her in the art studio—Rohit

'Every movement in art runs parallel with all the different forms of art, be it painting, theatre, cinema, architecture, literature or any other form. We have classic, gothic, Renaissance, modern, post-modern, de-con and contemporary styles in all of these art forms,' I say as the students listen to me, sitting on the bar stools in the studio. It's the usual kind of bunch—some are sleepy, some are fiddling with their pens, some are doodling in their notebooks and a few are listening eagerly.

'And all these art styles have existed all over the world,' Megha adds.

I nod in agreement. My first studio with her is going super. We are so much in sync that it's almost like performing a duet. I air my views on a topic and then she says something else completing it. It's like Frank Sinatra and Judy Garland singing together in divine harmony. We are by all means, a good team.

We finish the lecture and give a studio assignment to the students. It's a really interesting one—we put on cool music and ask the students to come in groups and dance to it as others quickly make free hand sketches of them in black ink with thick, flat or round brushes. Megha is swaying her head to the beat of the music. She seems to be really enjoying herself. I smile at her. She gets up and gestures me to join her. What is she suggesting? Is she asking me to dance with her? God no! There is no way I am doing that. I am the most terrible dancer. I dance like a cockroach. I panic.

She comes over, holds me by my hand and pulls me to stand up. I can't say no—it'll only create a scene. I will just go with her, do a couple of the dance moves I have seen Ranbir Kapoor do in the movies and come back. It's going be so quick that the students who are busy sketching will not even notice. As soon as I reach the dance floor and do the first move, I hear a sharp ear-piercing whistle. I look up and see Pranav giving me a thumbs-up. This is extremely embarrassing. I turn around like a robot and go back to my chair. I want to shrink and disappear. I want to hide under the chair. But what I can do is sit here as if I am super cool with everything and nothing even remotely awkward has happened.

The sketching exercise goes on for another hour. I outgrow the hot embarrassment I'd faced and we wrap up the studio.

'It was such a fun exercise! You've got some really good ideas,' Megha says as she helps me gather my books and notes.

'Thanks,' I smile, 'it's one of the coolest exercises that we did when we were in college.'

'Great. And you know, you have some really smooth dance moves. I'd love to dance with you some time.'

'Really? Thanks.' I am going to do my dance moves in front of the mirror tonight and see. Maybe I am not that bad after all!

'You are welcome,' she says as she tilts her head to a side. 'Can I have your phone number? I might need to call you when I sit down to prepare my next lecture with you.'

'Sure.' I give her my number and she leaves.

I look at her walking out of the door. Her walk is cool, a bit like Meg Ryan in *French Kiss*, that carefree, tomboyish kind of walk which has a bit of a charm to it. Just then I hear someone cough to catch my attention. I turn around and find Pranav standing there.

'Kya baat hai, sir-ji, exchanging numbers and all, haan?' he nudges me with his elbow.

'Pranav, please! I am your teacher here,' I say, embarrassed.

'Oh please, sir-ji, the class is over,' he whines. 'And, sir-ji, you should not look at her like that.'

Just then I get a chat alert from the Facebook messenger app on my phone. I look at the screen; it's that sex chat girl again—Saima. 'I bet you are thinking about sex right now.' I immediately delete the message and slide my phone back into my pocket.

'Arre, sir-ji? Getting *looove* messages from Megha ma'am already?'

'Shut up!'

'What shut up, sir-ji? I saw the two of you dancing. It was right out of one of those Hollywood romance dramas, floating on the clouds with the tender lightness of love and affection where the violin plays in the background as the lovers kiss each other.'

'Pranav!' Although what he is saying is tremendously offensive, I am kind of happy to hear how he explains it—like an art student. He has actually improved! Come to think of it, he's grown and learnt a lot within just a year. Last year he used to be so terrible with his work and expressions and concepts. And now he's become smart and quite confident about many things.

'Sir-ji, you have to stop all this or I will tell Nisha ma'am.'

'There is nothing *going on*! Shut up!'

'Okay, okay. But jokes apart, you know Megha ma'am's story, right?'

'What story? I don't know any story. I am tired and hungry. I want to go and eat something,' I say wearily.

'You don't know the story?' he asks with his eyes popping out. 'We call it "The Fat Dean's Hot Sex Affair". Although I know he is really fat and I really can't figure out how he can have sex, but anyway.'

Pranav has my complete attention. Food can wait a bit. 'What?'

'Haan. So the story goes like this. Years ago . . .' he starts. 'Actually, not years ago, it was only the year before last. I was just trying to make it sound more dramatic. Anyway. It was Megha ma'am's final year as a student in this college. She was one of those loser kids who come from a small village, have no sense of style and everyone calls them auntyji or behenji. She used to wear ill-fitting suits of terrible colours that would make even a blind person scream in agony. No one liked her. She was not even a good student. She used to fail most of the time. Everyone, including the stars and the blue sky high above, would wonder what the hell she was doing here when she did not have the slightest aptitude or talent for fine arts. But then, our fat boiled potato came along— Jabba the Hutt as you call him.

'He saw this girl and was smitten by her ugliness. Looking at him, I feel it's completely possible that what is beautiful to the world is ugly to him and vice versa. So he found this girl beautiful. They started spending a lot of time together. She would discuss all her projects with him for hours and blindly do whatever he asked her to do. She even went around saying that if you want to learn anything in life, make dean sir your *God* and all knowledge will come to you. This went on for a while, and eventually one thing led to another and they started having . . . er . . .' he lowered his voice to a whisper and said, '*s-e-x*! She would spend endless nights at his place and often come to college with him in his car. Soon the year came to an end and it was final thesis jury time. The external examiners came, looked at her work and thought it was worse than "ugly, fresh, wet shit". They wanted to fail her but the dean intervened in her viva like a super hero and tried to explain her concept and ideas. The externals shut him up and said "Let the student explain the design" and failed her anyway. And then—this is fantastic!—once the external examiners left, the dean asked the *college professors* to forge her marks in the list and make Megha ma'am top the thesis. Everyone knew she didn't really have any work but no one could say anything against the dean as he is the *authority*. So she not only passed but topped the thesis evaluation!'

'Bullshit. I don't believe you.' I think Pranav has some issues with Megha and this whole story is one of those rumours that get circulated so often that people actually start believing them.

'Listen to what happened after that,' Pranav continues, clearly not bothered by my comment. 'Megha ma'am went to do a master's degree in Mumbai. I have a friend there—I have friends everywhere—so I know what exactly happened.' He flaunts his inside knowledge. 'Ma'am was not able to cope with the studies and missed dean sir too much. She would call him up in the middle of the night, weep like a baby and tell him that she missed him and ask why he never visited her, complained that all the teachers hated her and picked on her all the time. Obviously! She had never worked hard a day in her life! Anyway, she was completely miserable there and finally left her two-year-long course only after a year and came back to be with the fat love of her life, and that is why she is here teaching us.'

'*Please!* All this is so not true! But I am really impressed with the story you made up. Staying with me, you are yourself becoming quite the storyteller.'

'You don't believe me?' he steps back and looks at me shell-shocked. 'I will call my friends, they will tell you.'

'Pranav, don't—'

'Ramona! Ishwin! Peetan!' he shouts out.

All three of them come and stand in front of me. I look at their faces, the same faces that I hated last year when I had started teaching here. But I feel so different looking at them now. I do not hate them any more. In fact, they are almost my friends.

'Guys, tell sir-ji, isn't the dean's hot sex affair with Megha ma'am true?' Pranav pokes.

They all laugh. 'Do we really need to say anything? Sir will know himself when he sees them together.'

Okay, I will.

19

**At times, writing about it is the best way to gain
strength and deal with it—Tara**

Her friends are now tired of listening to her sob stories. They
expect her to be over Tarun's death by now. They would never
say anything mean but she knows how they feel—there are
certain things that you can just sense.

It's another day for her at home when she doesn't have
anything to do. She doesn't know what to do. Sitting on her
bed, she picks up the remote control of the television and turns
it on. Some random movie is on. A man is lying on a recliner
and talking while a shrink sits next to him. After the man on
the recliner is done talking, the shrink says, 'You should write
down all your thoughts and feeling. It will give you a clearer
picture of what you are feeling and thinking, and clarity on
what you should do.'

Tara stares at the screen thinking hard. Is this a sign? Is this
her solution too? Would it help her improve her state of mind?
She gets up from her bed and opens the almirah that is full of

the presents Tarun had given her. There is a notebook he had given her once—a white notebook with the picture of a cute puppy on it. Tara pulls that notebook out, and sits down at her study table. She closes her eyes, takes a deep breath and starts to write.

What can you say about a twenty-one-year-old boy who died in his sleep?

20

When he goes to a grass and 'Lucy in the Sky with Diamonds' party he has no clue what's going on; learning never ends for some people—Rohit

Turns out that it was *the* party of the year! Really. It's all over the newspapers. I have a copy of the *Indian Times'* weekly supplement in front of me and I am looking at the coverage of the party the other night. There are pictures of everyone but me there. The monkey-like grinning face of Karun Mukharjee can be seen everywhere and with everyone. There is even a picture of that rich sculptor, Virath Seth. Oh look! Nisha is standing next to him in the picture. Everyone gets into the newspapers but me. There is a little story about Seth too. I read it quickly and learn nothing important about him other than that he is the richest artist in India, shuttles between India, London and Spain, hates Indian summers and is a bit of a player. Yes, he sleeps with most women he associates with. Maybe Nisha should stay away from him.

Right then Nisha comes and puts a cup of tea next to me on

the table. It's a warm, lazy September morning and the room is filled with the golden morning light. Pranav is still sleeping on the mattress in the living room with the painting he is working on next to him. Seems he fell asleep working. There are a couple of sparrows chirping on the window ledge— it's a beautiful love song kind of morning.

'Anything about the party in the magazine section?' Nisha asks casually.

'Anything? It's all over the paper. They even have a picture of you.'

'Really? Show me!'

I pass the paper to her and she smiles looking at her picture, 'Not bad!'

'So what did that Virath guy say? Did you talk to him?' I put an arm around her affectionately as she sits on the chair next to mine, a cup of tea in her hand.

'Yeah, it was wonderful talking to him actually. He seems to be a nice person. He said that he has had a project in his mind for a long time and is looking for a young artist to work with him. He said he would call me some time to discuss it,' Nisha says excitedly.

'Cool!' I act all normal. I don't want to kill this lovely moment by saying something that will result in an argument.

'I am so excited about it. This could be my chance to enter into the international art market after all these years . . .' she says with shining eyes. I force a smile, nod and kiss her on her forehead.

∿

'Are you sure you want to do this? Are you sure you want to go?' Nisha asks as I drive the car with Florence and the Machine playing in the background.

'Yeah, I mean what's the big deal? It's only a birthday party.'

'Yeah, but what concerns me is whose birthday party it is. All that history you have with him, that's what's going through my mind.'

'Yeah, but by going there I will be showing that I have let go of whatever happened in the past and want to start afresh now.'

Megha told me after the studio that it's Jabba's birthday today and she is throwing a party for him at his place and would love it if I would attend. So here we are—on the way to Jabba the Hutt's birthday party.

'Hmm, that's okay. But please don't overreact or create a scene if he says something mean.'

'What do you mean overreact or *create a scene*? When have I done that? I *never* create a scene!'

This is *so* not true! Why is she saying things like this? I am always calm and composed. I have total control over myself. I *never* overreact!

I keep turning to look at her, expecting a reply, while she changes the track on the music player until 'Heartlines' starts playing. I look at her again and she says, 'Will you just let me listen to this song? I like this song.' And starts to sway her head and sings the song along with her eyes closed, '*Just keep following the heart lines on your hand.*'

~

Loud crazy trance music is blaring out of giant speakers that could render most people deaf. It is a strange party, the likes of which I have never actually been to but only heard of or seen in movies and on TV. Seating on the floor is set along the walls with a low table in front where the guests are drinking and smoking. I turn and look at Nisha; I have not seen her so amused in ages—it looks like she'll burst into crazy laughter any instant.

'I didn't expect a party like this.' I whisper in her ear. I was expecting a more sophisticated gathering with wine and jazz music may be.

'This is so insane! I am so glad we came,' she whispers back.

'This place smells funny.'

'You bet it does!'

'There's so much smoke here I can hardly breathe.'

She laughs. 'Just stay around for a while and you will be doing more than just breathing.'

'What do you mean?'

What is wrong with Nisha? Why is she suddenly so excited?

'Nothing. Let's just mingle and meet people.'

'Hey! Rohit sir!' I hear someone call out my name loud. I look around and see a very happy Megha waving at me. She comes running to me and grabs me by the wrist. 'Come, let's dance.' She does a soft hip shake.

Oh man, this is awkward! I shoot a look of helplessness at Nisha. Struggling to control her laughter, she nods and waves at me, gesturing for me to go and dance with Megha.

I try to free my hand from Megha's grip, wiggling my wrist, 'But . . . I haven't even wished Ja— I mean the dean yet!'

'Oh that's okay,' Megha grabs my other wrist too. 'He is in the other room having *fun*. You can wish him later.' She drags me to the centre of the room, which is supposedly the dance floor and starts to move to the music. I stand in front of her in a panic, trying to figure out what to do.

'Come on, Rohit sir, *dance*!' she instructs laughingly, then suddenly turns her back towards me, does a quick hip shake and jumps around again to face me. She takes both my hands and puts them on her shoulders. Feeling like a monkey clinging to a tree branch, I fight the urge to smile as I do the one-two-one-two footwork that I had learnt ages ago at the salsa workshop that Nisha had forced me to attend.

'That's my boy!' She says coming close to me. Something is wrong with her—she does not seem to be like her normal self. 'Come on now, do this with me,' she says as she hops around again and starts to shake her hip again. This is it; this is my big chance to run away. I instantly dash away and hide myself among a group of guests sitting on one of the floor arrangements along the wall. I look at them and nod graciously with a smile, ignoring the confused, questioning looks they give me.

This is a really weird party. Everyone looks strange here. I look at the people sitting next to me from the corner of my eye like Sherlock to see what they are doing. One of them has a tiny bowl in his hand and is mixing some kind of stuff that looks like dry tea leaves. I get up and look around for Nisha when someone taps me on my shoulder.

It's Nisha.

'What the hell is happening here? Why does everyone seem completely crazy?' I am shocked and starting to get a bit dizzy myself.

'God! Don't tell me you still haven't got it!'

What does she mean? What is it that I am supposed to get?

'It's a weed party!' she whispers, lowering her head.

Oh my Fu@#$ng Lord!

'You mean like a *drugs* party?' My jaw drops so far that Nisha almost sets it close with her hands.

She nods, suppressing her laughter, 'Your dean is some dude, man!'

I look around once again to see all the guests in this trance set-up. There are even some students here. I see two of Pranav's friends—Ishwin and Peetan—sitting in a corner and giggling to each other.

'God! This is terrible! We've got to get out of here!'

'Hey, Rohit sir!' It's Megha again as she comes to me running and grabs hold of my wrist again, 'Come on, let's dance.' She does the same dance move again. She is repeating herself; she is definitely high; I can slip out by being a little smart.

'Hey, how are you? I have been looking for you for like an hour now!' I say.

'What?' she frowns.

'Yeah, actually we were leaving so . . . I wanted to say bye.'

'No, sir, you are not leaving.' She shakes her head and stamps her feet like a baby.

'I have to go . . . some place else.' I try to free my wrist by pushing her hand away.

'No,' she whines and slumps on to the floor.

'Megha, child, I've got to go. I will see you tomorrow in college.'

'Okay,' she suddenly gets up, 'but you have to promise me something.'

'What?'

'Me and dean sir are going on a trip to Kasol the next weekend. You have to come with us.'

'I will see.' I smile

'No, no, no!' Megha stamps her foot again.

'Okay, okay. I will come. I'll see you at college.'

'Okay!' she says, sounding immensely happy and gives me a little peck on my lips. I pull my head back in utter shock.

~

We are back in the car and driving home in silence. It was all quite awkward at the party. How can the dean be so cool with students using drugs in his house? I know some people don't consider weed drugs, but for the dean to serve it to his students and indulge with them? That is a bit much!

'Virath called, by the way.' Nisha finally breaks into my thoughts as she fiddles with the music player in the car.

'What did he say?' It's best to talk about something other than what's going on in my head.

'He sounded quite excited about the project he mentioned at the party. It's a series of sculptures he wants to do. He wants to meet and discuss the projects. He is in Kerala these days, said he'll send air tickets soon . . . maybe some time next to next week or something.'

This guy is something else! If he is really not that big a pervert then why would the papers label him so? Still, I don't think it's good to bring this up right now; I am driving and I get distracted very easily.

'Are you going?' I can ask at least this much.

'Of course I am going!' Nisha looks at me with eyes as big as saucers, 'It is the biggest chance I have ever got in my career so far.'

'Okay. I guess if you are going to Kerala then I can go with Megha and Jabba to Kasol. Their trip is also around that time.'

Nisha smiles, 'Megha is a funny girl though. Be careful with her.'

'Yeah, I know,' I laugh, 'I can handle her.'

Silence

'And I don't like that Virath guy much. There were funny things about him in the newspaper today. You be careful around him too.'

Nisha does not say anything and finally a song plays on the music player: 'Turning Tables' by Adele.

Music drowns our words but not our thoughts.

21

Books by four authors reach the office that other authors only dream of and some would kill for—Ravi Kapoor

He has never spent much of his time at home. Even now, when most people his age prefer to spend a 'peaceful' retired life at home, he gets dressed early in the morning every day and arrives in his office at his production house at precisely 8.30 and waits for the daily newspaper. For decades, the entertainment section of these newspapers and magazines have talked about him and never tired. At times he has had to pay them and at times they have wanted to write stories about him on their own. It amuses him how the media is always interested in what he is up to. He has only just announced the idea of making a big film based on a new novel with his son upon his return from Prague and the 'news' has already made headlines. Either the PR department of his production house is very active or the common man considers him the god of Hindi films and is always keen to know what he has to offer next.

He has had a dedicated team of assistants working for him for many years and even he cannot deny the fact that what he has become today, the pinnacle he has reached, would not have been possible without them. But he seldom expresses his gratitude for them. He believes that if you are soft with your employees, they will not work hard enough—dominance and authority are some of the principles that he has always practised and most of all now, when he is expanding his 'empire' for his son. He has started recruiting young and more enthusiastic professionals—ones who will understand and relate to the new ideas his son will bring. One such fresh recruit is Tahir Kashyup. With bright dazzling dreams of his own to make it big in this world, Tahir is as dedicated and hard-working as anyone can be. Every morning he reaches the office before Ravi Kapoor, lays the newspapers on the table in Kapoor's office and waits for him at his desk. Kapoor is not unaware of Tahir's potential, hard work and dedication, and that is why he always gives him double the work that he gives anyone else. Kapoor has always believed that the only way to make a man shine is by helping him realize that he has far greater potential than he is aware of, and the only way to do that is by performing more than one can ever imagine. Tahir knows that Ravi Kapoor considers him special. And his burning ambition pushes him even harder to work more and impress his boss with his performance and dedication. And that is why in less than a week, he has done the market survey for what is hot and what is not for the Indian youth of today on the literary front. In the last five years, a new genre of books has sprouted that is not only being read by the school- and college-going crowd but also by mature readers. Most of these light short novels are the authors' own stories, which many critics have started to talk about. Some hail them as 'Reality Fiction' and others trash them on the basis of their imperfect language but no one can deny the fact that these books sell more copies in India than the 'acclaimed' national and international literary authors of the time. Tahir has found out that Vikram Rawat is the undisputed king and the pioneer of this genre of books, had familiarized over hundred books and read a total of fifteen books in the past one week.

After Ravi Kapoor arrives, Tahir waits for one hour, which is precisely the time that Kapoor takes to read the newspaper, and then goes to his office with the four books he has shortlisted. He has talked to his colleagues about the selection of the books and none of them differed or opposed his choice.

He waits at the door to Kapoor's office for him to acknowledge his presence. 'Good morning, sir.'

Ravi Kapoor looks at him and gestures for him to come in.

Tahir walks to his table, 'Sir, I have shortlisted four books from the bestsellers in the market these days.'

Ravi Kapoor takes off his glasses and gives him a sharp look.

'All these authors are popular among the youth and the stories have the potential to be developed into commercial Hindi films,' Tahir continues.

'Which one is your favourite?'

Tahir smiles. He has a clear choice in mind but he will not reveal it. He wants to know which one Ravi Kapoor would choose, so he himself can learn and understand from Kapoor's judgment. 'All of them are my favourites, sir; that is why I have brought them to you.' In a way, this is not a lie.

Ravi Kapoor nods and return his attention to the file in front of him. This is the cue for Tahir to leave the books on the table and leave.

Tahir places the short pile of the four books on the table and leaves. The four names, out of which the fate and destiny of one might change forever, are Vikram Rawat, Jeet Obiroi, Rohit Sehdev and Karun Mukharjee.

22

If you do not win an award, you are a nobody
—Karun

Dear Karun,

We at 'We are for the Writers' got your reference from one of our writer friends and are thrilled to get in touch with you. We are a one-stop-shop for all your needs as an author. Apart from providing excellent editing services, the other services we provide include critical reviews and suggestions for submitted manuscripts and copy-editing. We are also a literary agency and can negotiate really great publishing deals for you. Our list of esteemed clients includes major award-winning authors of our time like Vikram Rawat. For your reference, we are attaching a sample edit from Rawat's

```
second book. We look forward to hearing from
you.
    Cheers,
    Subodh Sharma
```

Huh! Got my reference from a friend, my ass! If that had been true then they would have sent me the mail on my personal email account and not the one that I have made exclusively for my fan mail. I am sure their editing service is going be worse than pig shit; I can offer *them* my editing services, which will be a thousand times better than theirs. Anyway, they said they have worked for Vikram Rawat. If that is true then they definitely will have contacts I can use so I should stay in touch. Award-winning author, he says. Damn! It is actually very important to win an award these days. The Popular Book Awards are a bit too far away. I need to find another way to win an award. But that is for later. Let me just reply to this asshole right now.

```
Dear Subodh,
    Thank you so much for getting in touch.
You do sound like a one-stop-shop for all
authors. Can you please share a detailed list
of your esteemed authors with me? Looking
forward to working with you.
    Best,
    Karun
```

23

**When the hot sex affair of the Fat Potato is revealed!
And when Rohit hides and watches the music video
Coz your sex takes me to paradise dedicated to him
—Rohit**

I seriously need to get over my illusion that the world is all flowers and roses and everyone has their ethics in place. I am on my way home after the disastrous trip with Megha and the dean and I am still in shock from the things I saw.

I reach my apartment and ring the bell.

Pranav opens the door. 'Sir-ji! Welcome back.' He shakes my hand.

'Thank you.' I force a smile and put my red rucksack on the floor next to the wall. I enter the living room and see Nisha and Ramona, Pranav's girlfriend, sitting together; they smile at me. I go and sit next to Nisha and kiss her on the forehead. There is no greater joy than coming back home and kissing the one you love most. It gives you a kind of peace, a sense of security that makes you feel everything is all right, and that if everything

were to fall apart, you'd have your home to come back to. I put
my arm around Nisha and kiss her on her cheek.

'What?' she looks at me surprised.

I smile at her, 'Nothing,' I say and kiss her again. I don't care
much about Ramona and Pranav being there.

'God!' she rolls her eyes.

I hear Pranav clearing his throat and when I look at him he
starts to look around as if he has not seen anything.

'So, sir-ji, tell us . . . how was your trip?' he has the trace
of a naughty smile on his face. I think he probably knows the
things I have seen.

'Don't ask, yaar, don't ask.' I shake my head.

'Why? What happened?' He acts all innocent as if he does
not know anything.

Okay, he seriously needs to give up this act! Yes, he was right
about the dean and Megha. *I get it!*

'What happened? Tell us.' Nisha squeezes my hand and smiles
at me while Pranav puts his arm around Ramona, struggling to
suppress his laughter. I think he would have wanted to hide his
relationship with her for some more time but right now he is too
excited to realize where his hand is going and where he is sitting
till I unknowingly stare at his hand on Ramona's shoulder and
he pulls it back at lightning speed.

'It was, by far, the worst trip I have ever been on.' I start, 'First
of all when I say they fight, it is an understatement. They yell at
each other, louder than normal human beings are capable of, *in
public*! God! It was so embarrassing. We stopped at this roadside
dhaba on our way up to have tea. Apparently, Jabba has diabetes,
so he is not supposed to have any sugar, but the tea that came

had sugar in it. Megha was furious; she refused to talk to Jabba. That's when it started, and within minutes it went outrageously out of control. They were yelling things like "This tea will pass your lips only over my dead body!" and "If you won't talk to me then I will drink this tea in one gulp!"

'Oh my God! Really? Even teenagers don't behave like that these days!' Nisha's eyes widen with excitement.

'Yes, and they were yelling like I have never heard people yell before, at a dhaba with so many people around. I actually got up and hid behind a car after a while so that people would not think I'm with them.

'And that was not all. When we reached Kasol and checked into the hotel, we took a double bedroom with an extra bed. It had just rained and was a bit chilly. As soon as we entered the room, Megha said she really needed a shower and went into the bathroom. Five minutes later, she came out in a pair of hot pants which weren't even visible under the long T-shirt she was wearing on top. It seemed like she did not have anything on other than that white T-shirt and the black bra she was wearing under it.'

'Oh my God!' Pranav gasped and Ramona gave him an angry nudge.

Maybe I should not be talking about all this in front of them but I am really frustrated and need to get it out.

'Jabba took one look at Megha and fell on the bed on his tummy, which was curious because I had never thought that someone as fat as him could lie on his tummy like that. Anyway, after a few seconds he said, "Meghu, baby, please come and lie here next to me," patting the space next to him on the bed.'

'Good Lord!' Nisha's excitement has turned into shock.

'Yes. And that was all I could take. I got up after that and said I was going to the restaurant to have coffee if anyone wanted to join me. Obviously no one did and I went out by myself. When I came back, they were sleeping in each other's arms.'

'Sir-ji, now do you believe me?' Pranav says with a sense of victory.

'Yes, you were right! Now go distribute chocolates in the whole city,' I retort, irritated.

'No, I am not going distribute chocolates in the whole city,' he laughs, 'but I will go and drop Ramona home and come back in half an hour.'

'Okay,' I say as he and Ramona get up and leave.

Pranav shuts the door behind him.

To think of it, the trip was not that bad actually. While Megha and Jabba were busy licking each other all over, I got quite some time to work on my novel. In fact, I am almost done with it now. I just need to re-read the last chapter I wrote and send it to the online editor I have hired. I think I should work on it after relaxing a bit.

There is silence in the room. I look at Nisha, who is staring at the floor with unseeing eyes.

I put my arm around her shoulders and hug her. 'What happened?'

She slowly shakes her head.

'Come on, tell me.'

Finally, she looks up at me. 'I met Tara again today. Remember the girl I told you about? Meetali's friend?'

'Yes, yes. Of course I remember her. What happened to her?'

'She's still struggling with her grief. I wish I could help her somehow. She has started writing her story, about the pain she is suffering. I hope she completes writing her story and gets it published. Do you think we can help her get published?'

'Nisha, I understand your concern, but I don't think there is anything you can do actually. No one can know what she is going through right now. She will have to gather her strength and come out of it on her own.' I hug her and kiss her on her forehead.

'I know,' she says without looking at me.

'How was your trip?' I ask, trying to distract her. I want her to think about other things.

'It was okay. We had a lengthy discussion about the project for a day.' She does sound tired too.

'That is good. What is the project?'

'He wants to do a series on Indian women from various regions, focusing on their different figures and features.'

'That sounds interesting.'

'Yeah, but the only problem is that he wants to sculpt these women partially in the nude so he can catch their sexuality as well. I don't know how the government and the politicians are going react to him representing our heritage in this manner!'

'Oh.' He is making nudes. This is how he gets close to all the women. This is how entices them and then sleeps with them! But I must not let my apprehensions show. It's only going to result in a fight.

'Anyway, let's go sleep. I am really tired,' she groans.

'Actually, I want to sit and write for a while.'

We go to our room and she gets ready for bed while I wait for my laptop to start up.

'You know something? I don't like this Megha girl much. She might be in love with the dean but there is a decency one must maintain,' Nisha says as she ties her hair in a bun.

'I know, I am keeping my distance from her.'

Silence.

'I don't like this Virath guy much either. I have a feeling that his intentions are not all pure.' There! I have said it! *I have to warn her!*

'What do you mean?' she turns to look at me. She does not look happy.

'I mean . . . you know . . . the other day, the newspaper said all sorts of things about him and now he wants to make these semi-nudes with you . . .'

'God! I seriously can't believe you just said that! You call yourself an artist? You are so narrow-minded!'

'I just—'

'Please, Rohit, I am not having this discussion.' She turns her back towards me.

This is not how we sleep generally. She always puts her head on my shoulder and looks at my laptop screen for a while, reading what I type until she falls asleep. We might even get up in the night and make love.

I have made her very angry tonight. But is it really my fault? Can't she see what that guy is actually up to? And shouldn't she be feeling good about my protectiveness?

I open my email to check if I have got any important messages before I start writing. There is one mail from someone called *hornygirlforhornyboys*. God! Is this the sex chat girl again? I open the mail and read:

```
It's the middle of the night and I can't stop
thinking about you. The mere thought of you
sexes me up and I get horny. So this is what
I did, I shot a little video for you. Check
out the attachment.
```

God! Has she sent me a sex video? Dancing in the nude? I download the attachment, plug in my earphones and play the video.

The snappy music starts and then the girl appears, her face covering most of the screen, and starts lip-syncing the lyrics, '*Oh yeah, yeah, yeah!*' as she bobs her head to the beat, her eyes shut as if she is totally lost in the music.

Then she steps back and shows her full self. She is wearing skimpy blue clothes with white stripes that accentuate the curves of her body. What she is wearing does not qualify as a dress actually. Lingerie maybe.

'*And you make me feel like, locked out of heaven,*' she sings with her mouth wide open as she dances, running around on the screen. She does dance well.

'*And your sex takes me to pa-ra-dise coz your sex takes me to pa-ra-dise and it shooow-wooo-wooo-wooos*' She thrusts her hips from side to side and then she pulls out a life-size picture of me, hugs it, kisses it, licks it from head to toe and starts dancing with it and runs around with it. The whole thing is actually quite hilarious.

'So this is your idea of a *not* nude?'

It's Nisha. When did she wake up? I'm completely embarrassed.

'Nisha . . . I . . .' I want to tell her that I hadn't meant to continue, that I hadn't taken it seriously, but nothing comes out.

24

You have to bear your tragedies alone—Tara

To the world it seems that she has gone into hibernation. She refuses to come out of her room and almost never steps out of the house. Many have declared that she has lost her mind and has not been able to bear the loss of her love. But in reality, something different has been happening. In reality, she has been working really hard, harder than she has ever worked on anything in her life. She has been typing like a machine for the past two months, so much so that most of the letters on the keyboard of her computer have worn off.

She types the last words of her story: *And then I did something that I had never done in front of her before. I put my arms around my mother and I cried.*

She stares at the screen as the cursor blinks rhythmically, like her heart, next to the full stop. She has poured her heart into this story. All she wants to do now is to cry, to weep bitterly, louder than she has ever wept before. But she doesn't. She just stares at the cursor on the screen, unblinkingly, as a single, lonely tear rolls down her cheek.

25

And now he can hatch his evil plot—Karun

```
Dear Karun,
    Thank you so much for your reply. We are
delighted to hear from you and very excited
to work with you. Please check out our
website www.weareforthewriters.com to see
the various offers we have for our authors
and choose the one that suits you the best.
Also please find attached the list of our
esteemed clients.
    We look forward to hearing from you soon.
    Cheers!
    Subodh Sharma
```

Huh! Check you out my ass. Just look at him . . . telling me to buy a package from him. Anyway, let me just see the list of his 'esteemed clients' that he keeps boasting about.

Who says God is dormant?! Just look at this list. Right now, this is the best thing that could have ever happened. This is the most brilliant piece of information I have come across in a long, long time. I can't believe my eyes: Rohit Sehdev's name is in the list of clients. This is just the thing I need to destroy Rohit *forever*! THIS IS FREAKING BRILLIANT! I've got to tell Mr Dé about it right now!

```
Dear Sir,
    I must meet you as soon as possible. Please
let me know the earliest we can meet—I have
hit the JACKPOT!
    Best,
    Karun
```

26

She has found her courage, she has found her strength—Tara

It is for the first time in two months that she has come out with her friends. Her friends and relatives used to visit her at home but she did not talk to them much; she had a storm brewing in her heart and her head. But now, having written down her story, she understands what had happened to her. It was almost as if she has stepped out of the whole situation and is looking at it from an outsider's perspective. Tarun has left her, forever. And she will never stop missing him. At times the pain of his absence, the desperation to get him back will be so strong that she will just break down and cry. But then she will gather herself, take a deep breath, wipe her tears and stand up again. It's true what they say—what doesn't kill you only makes you stronger. She has survived the loss of the love of her life and has come out stronger than before. She is sitting at a coffee shop with her friends, laughing and smiling. And these are not those fake smiles that she would paste on her face to make people around her believe she was okay. These were the kinds of smiles that were coming from her heart.

'We are really glad you came with us today.' Tara's friend, Veena, says, lightly squeezing her hand affectionately.

Her cousin Meetali was also there with her friend Nisha.

'Thank you,' Tara smiles, 'I had forgotten for a while how Tarun always said that no matter what, he always wants to see me happy.' She has become more vocal about her feelings; she is not ashamed of them any more. 'I have been through some tough times,' she continues 'and I think I am still not completely out of them, but I have learned to handle them.'

'You have been very brave, Tara. It takes a lot of courage for what you have done. It's not easy to bare your feeling in a story like you have.' Nisha has read what Tara has written; she cried at almost every page while she was reading it. 'You look a lot better today. I am very relieved to see you looking happy.'

Tara smiles, 'They say that you never really stop loving someone. You either never loved them or you always will.' Tara looks at Veena with shining eyes, 'And you know, while writing my story, I also realized that I am not the only one in this world who is going through such pain. A lot of people experience such pain and agony. And that is why I want to share my story with the world. So that anyone going through such heartache can find solace in my book. I want to get my story published.'

'I think you absolutely should! And if you need any help, let me know. Rohit is a published author and I am sure he will be able to help you.' Nisha hands over Rohit's business card to Tara.

'Thank you so much but I am going to try on my own first. I want to take my story out to the world so that people can read it and know that when you lose someone you love, you have to take care of yourself even more; you have to love yourself even more and keep yourself happy. Because that is the only thing people who love you want for you. And that is the only way you can keep their love alive and in turn, keep them alive in your heart. I want to get this published because I never want Tarun to die; I want to make him immortal.'

27

Someone's life is (finally) about to change
—Ravi Kapoor

They say that you can never have both; you can either be successful in your career or you can have a happy family life.

Sitting in his office, Ravi Kapoor is the king of his world. As a youth in his twenties, this was all he wished for. And now, when his wish has come true, he is missing something else. He is missing a family, a wife with whom he could sit and discuss his worries and anxieties, a son who will sit by his side and expand his empire further. Though he has a son, and a wife, they are so distant from him. It is the price Ravi Kapoor has paid for what the world calls success.

But he knows how to silence these desires and dissatisfactions and focus on his work—it is something he has learned over years of hard work and dedication.

It has taken him three days to read all the four books and one more day to decide which one he wants to base his next film on. He had made notes for each of the books and put them systematically in a file. He is looking for a simple story of an ordinary boy that has an honest charm to it that depicts the feelings and thoughts of the day's youth. Rohit Sehdev's *Those Things in Life Big and Small* comes closest to what he is looking for. Though he hates the title, he has made up his mind about the book. He will ask his assistant, Tahir, to get in touch with the author and settle the deal for the film rights of the book.

He puts the book on the top of the pile, closes his eyes and leans back in the chair. He is tired and his eyes burn. With age he has lost his stamina to work long hours and today, he feels even more tired than usual. A bit feverish too. He hates leaving office in the middle of the day unless it is for work but today his body is demanding rest and he does not have the energy to deny it like he used to in his youth. Taking a deep breath, he packs his papers in his briefcase and gets up to leave for home. All of a sudden his head reels; he feels nauseated and there is a searing pain in his chest. Then he falls and the world blacks out for him.

28

So Megha is a junkie, a junkie teacher—Rohit

Funny orders I got from Jabba the Hutt today. Megha is no longer to take the studio class with me. Apparently, there is a shortage of faculty and we cannot afford to spare two teachers for one studio any more; Megha will teach the other section of first year students since the teacher taking that class has resigned and left the job without notice. What I hear is that he left in a huff because his 1.5-lakh-rupee camera was stolen from his apartment inside the university campus and the security department refused to help him find out who stole it. Anyway, it's kind of nice that I am not teaching with Megha any more because Nisha has already started to have issues with her and after the dancing girl episode I don't want to do anything to upset her. Nisha had burst into angry screaming and shouting when she saw me watching the sexy home-made video. Although I was able to calm her down, something between us had changed that night.

I enter the studio and put my bag on the table and look

around. It's a usual day for the students—some are sitting in a group next to the window, chatting; others are working with their canvases on their easels and earphones in their ears, listening to music; a handful are eating lunch and gossiping and there are a few who are doing nothing.

I am about to take a round and see what progress the students have made with their projects and hold discussions with them when Pranav spots me and comes running.

'Sir-ji! You know what happened?' He is jumping with excitement.

'What?' I ask, setting my papers and books on the table without looking at him—I want to appear all busy and important.

'You know Megha ma'am teaches art history and criticism, no?'

'Yes.'

'And you know how she just comes and keeps copying from the textbook and writing on the blackboard without really teaching or explaining anything.'

I nod.

'You know what she did today?'

'What?' I look at him; he is so excited that his eyes might pop any instant.

'*She came to class totally stoned.*' He stresses on each word as he whispers.

'Nonsense! What is wrong with you? Stop making up such stupid stories and go to your seat and work.' I say in a flat, mechanical voice. I must sound serious and completely non-gossipy; I am his *teacher*.

'*Sir-ji, I am telling you. She must have taken some serious junk*,' he whispers again, stressing each word. '*Her eyes were red! I saw that when I went to ask her if I could go to the toilet once the class ended.*'

That is so lame. He is a final year student and he goes and asks the teacher if he can go to the toilet *after* the class is over. And maybe he is right, maybe she did come to the class with a hangover. After the things I have seen on the trip and at that party, this is actually nothing.

'She also yelled at Ramona without any reason. She was totally out of her senses and did not even know what she was saying. She asked Ramona about *Starry Night* by Van Gogh and when Ramona answered it correctly, she started yelling that it was not the answer and that was not what she had asked her, again and again—*thrice*. The whole class was shocked.'

'Okay, nice story.' I pretend not to believe him, 'Will you go back to work? I am going to talk to each student and discuss their projects.'

'And, sir-ji,' he nudges me with his elbow, a conspiratorial look in his eyes, 'I'm telling you the Fat Potato sent Megha ma'am to teach the other section,' he says with his usual naughty expression, 'because he is feeling threatened by you!' He winks.

I cannot believe what I'm hearing but there is a possibility because of the way Megha was falling all over me in the party.

29

The rains of Dwindle-Do—Tara

All they're publishing these days are stories of horny boys and horny girls who only look at each other's tits and butts. Tara is at a bookstore and the bookshelves are lined with titles like *How I Had Sex for the First Time*, *The Bastard and the Bitches*, *Shag Me in the End* and the like. She is appalled to see these books and even more enraged to see many youngsters picking them up and opening random pages, giggling and then going to the cash counters to get the books billed. She has written a story about her deepest love, how she lost it and how she found the strength to live on through that love. And no one wants to publish her story. She has sent the manuscript to so many publishers that she has lost count. 'It does not have that commercial quality,' some said. Other replies were the standard ones that read as if they were auto-generated by a computer system: 'We are sorry but your manuscript does not suit our current publishing plan' or 'Thank you for sending us your manuscript but we are not looking for any manuscript submissions right now'. Having tried the email submission route, she's decided to personally meet one of the publishers. She had sent a hard copy of her manuscript to them and they have not replied yet. She wants to ask them if they intend to publish her. She has had enough.

She pulls out her cell phone and looks at the time—1 p.m. It's an odd time to go to an office since it will be lunch time soon. She decides to wait in the bookstore a bit more. She peeps out of the window and looks at the sky. Dark clouds are building up.

~

The man sitting in the reception in Dash Publishers has made her wait three hours before finally sending her to meet the editor. Dash started as a very small publication house a few years ago but today it is the biggest player when it comes to popular fiction in India. If Tara's manuscript is accepted by this publisher, the book will surely do well.

It is pouring cats and dogs outside accompanied by the occasional clap of thunder every now and then. Something is making her feel small and weak and she cannot figure out the reason. She opens the door and stands there. The editor is busy working on his computer. He glances at her and then returns his attention to the screen in front of him.

'Yes, come,' is all he utters.

She walks in and sits on the chair in front of his table. After a few seconds, he looks away from the computer screen and turns to her, 'Yes, tell me what you want.'

'Sir, I had sent my manuscript for your consideration. I hope you liked it. I wanted to know if there's a possibility of being published with you.' For some reason, what she is saying sounds lame to her too.

The editor rolls his eyes, '*Seriously?* Is that all you wanted to see me for? Is that why you created a scene outside? Girl, get real, *please.* Is there anything else you want to ask or talk about?'

She only sits there, bewildered. She does not know what to say. After a few seconds of hesitation, she says, 'Sir, I just want to know if you have taken any decisions about my manuscript.'

'Listen *carefully*, girl, because I am not going to repeat myself. You see that pile of manuscripts lying there?' he says, pointing to a huge stack of spiral-bound manuscripts haphazardly lying in the corner of the room. 'We get hundreds of manuscripts every month. Every Teenu, Meenu, Cheenu out there thinks he's Shakespeare and is writing these days. And do you know what kind of writing it is, girl?' He stands up, violently, pushing his chair back, picks up a manuscript from the pile, flips a few pages and hands it her, 'Here, this. Just read this.' He says as he puts the open manuscript in front of her.

Tara sits there like a stone. She does not know what to do.

'Okay, I will read it for you.' He picks up the manuscript and starts to read out loud, '*She was sitting in front of me in the moving train and she was so HOT. I wanted to rip her jeans off, pour chocolate sauce on her nice round ass and lick it—yum, yum, yum.*' He looks up angrily. 'This guy is talking about a girl's ass. This is ugly!' he says as he holds up the manuscript and shakes it. 'This is the kind of writing I am subjected to. And you think you have the right to just barge into my office, and ask me, all doe-eyed, if I liked your manuscript? *Fine!* I will look at your manuscript right now and tell you if I like it,' he snaps. 'Your name is Tara, right?' He walks back to the pile of manuscripts, finds the one with her name and comes back to sit on his chair.

He opens the manuscript and begins to read the synopsis out loud, 'This is the story of a young girl who blah, blah, blah . . . and then she lost her love blah, blah, blah . . . and then how finally she finds the strength to live. You know, Tara? We've all read tragic love stories and, honestly, we do not want to read them all over again. This is just that same sad, old thing again. We will not be interested in publishing this.' He flings the manuscript back on to the heap. 'You can leave now,' he says and turns back to the computer screen.

Tara gets up, walks to the door, pushes it open and leaves. Anger is building inside her. The farther she walks from the editor's office, the angrier she feels. Finally, she steps out of the building and into the crazy pouring rain. She has tears rolling down her eyes but they are lost in the rain. She walks on. She is soaked to the skin by now. Her wet hair is pasted to the sides of her face and her shoes are filled with water. She is angry. Raging mad. She has never felt such fury in her entire life. She wants to scream and shout. That editor had no right to behave with her the way he did. If he did not want to publish her manuscript, he should have simply said so. Why did he humiliate her the way he did? She refuses to take this humiliation. In the pouring rain, she turns around and walks back to the office of Dash Publishers, this time with firm and determined steps.

She enters the Dash office. She does not ask for anyone's permission and directly goes into the editor's office.

'I want my manuscript back. Give me back my manuscript!' she says authoritatively, as though she owns the place.

'We do not have any such policy.' The editor does not look at her and continues working on his computer.

She keeps standing there and does not budge.

'We do not have any such policy,' the editor repeats, 'Now please get off my carpet and leave, you are spoiling it. God! I will have to send it to the dry-cleaner's now. You have got mud all over it.'

Instead of walking to the door, Tara walks up to the editor. She stands there and looks at him for a few seconds, her anger building up even higher. And suddenly, just like that, she slaps him hard across his face, leaving him flabbergasted. Then she picks up her manuscript from the corner of the room, hugs it tightly to her chest and leaves the room.

30

The rains of Dwindle-Do II—Karun

I don't understand why it has to rain! I mean I know why it rains but it's such a terrible thing. Imagine water falling on you from the sky, making you wet and just disrupting your whole routine. Who needs this fucking rain? The roads are all clogged with muddy water right now and the simple act of going to Mr Dé's office has become a mission.

I finally reach my destination and pay the autowallah before I get off so that the money does not get wet. As I run into the office building, I see an angry girl walking out with long determined strides. She has a spiral-bound file in her hands and her eyes are fixed ahead. She looks stark raving mad right now and is heading in my direction. If I don't get out of her way, she might just bulldoze me!

I step aside just in time and she passes me by, straight into the pouring rain. She seems to be lost in her own world with no idea about what is happening around her. Fucking crazy she seems.

The guy at the reception informs Mr Dé that I am here and tells me that I can go inside.

'Come in, Karun, come in,' Mr Dé greets me as I enter.

I smile and sit on the chair in front of him.

'You are wet,' he says. 'Would you like to change into some dry clothes? Truly, you look so wet . . .' He leans forward and puts his hand on my chest, 'See, your shirt is all wet.'

'No, sir, it's fine.' I smile.

'Take off your shirt. I will get a dry shirt for you.'

Okay, this is awkward. I don't want to offend him. He is my publisher after all. If I piss him off he might just ruin my career. Maybe I should just do as he says. What's the big deal anyway?

He is looking at me hopefully when the phone on his desk suddenly starts to ring.

'One minute,' he says and picks up the phone. 'Hello?'

The person on the other end of the line is almost yelling and I can hear most of what he's saying. I think it's Mr Dé's editor. He sounds very upset. It's almost like he is crying and is saying 'How can she do this?' over and over again. I am sure something dramatic has happened in the office but honestly, right now I don't care much about it. I have a much bigger plan in mind to hatch. I sit there, listening to the thunder outside, while Mr Dé tries to calm the editor down. But the man just won't calm down so finally, Mr Dé says, 'I will do something about it. Right now I am in a meeting. I will talk to you later, okay?' and puts the phone down.

He looks at me and smiles, but before he can say anything, I jump up, 'Sir! I have hit a gold mine! No wait, not a gold mine, a *diamond* mine!'

'Really?' he chuckles, 'What is it?'

'I have figured out which editing service Rohit has hired to edit his next book.'

He smiles and looks at me, 'So?'

'This is our big chance, sir! This is our big chance to destroy him.'

'How?'

'I just need to hack into the email account of that editing service and download his manuscript. Once we have that, we can publish it under someone else's name or just make up a pen name and publish with that. Once the book is published, he will be doomed! I just need to get my hands on that manuscript now.'

This is a brilliant plan! He's got to agree to it.

'My dear Karun, I have been in this business since before you even knew how to wipe the snot off your nose.'

I frown. What the fuck does he mean?

'You are a bit late,' he continues as he puts a spiral-bound bundle of A4 sheets on the table and gives a wicked smile. 'I already have the manuscript.'

I look back at him, bewildered. This man is amazing! Epic awesome! My respect for him has just quadrupled! I could actually give him a hand job for this!

'It seems that you have forgotten,' he looks at me with the same wicked smile, 'that they are also a literary agency, and I am a publisher.'

31

The rains of Dwindle-Do III—Rohit

The rain is falling in sheets. The weather has become so unpredictable these days; it's like totally mad. I park my car and run to my apartment building in the heavy downpour. My shoes are so wet that they sprout water when I take a step. I take the elevator to my apartment and ring the bell. Nisha opens the door.

'God! You are all wet!'

'Yeah,' I enter and take off my shoes. I am almost feeling cold in this crazy September summer. 'Really crazy weather and you won't believe what happened at college today.'

'What?'

'There is something seriously wrong with the dean, man! I mean, what I saw today was totally insane.' I shake my head.

'Why?' Nisha laughs. 'Did they start dancing naked in the corridors today? That would have been a very ugly sight though—Jabba: naked. Yuck!'

'It was worse than that, Nisha, it was far worse than that.'

God! I am still so irritated.

'Well, you can tell me all about it while you change out of your wet clothes,' Nisha insists.

We walk into and bedroom together and as I pull out fresh clothes, I explain, 'One of the faculty members has left college without giving notice and they are finding it tough to adjust classes and the teachers. So instead of two teachers in the studio class I was taking, there'll only be one teacher—me—and Megha has been shifted to another section.'

'Okay.'

I take off my shirt and wipe myself with a towel. 'I had some free time after lunch today so Jabba called me to his office and asked me to go the studio Megha was talking and help her out as she was facing some problems. I am sure he must not have had any other option or he would never have sent me to her studio. I went there, Nisha, and you won't believe what I saw.'

'What?'

'That girl, Megha! She does not know anything! God! She had to teach them a simple wash technique to use water colours and she just couldn't do it! When I reached, she had already wasted some five sheets and was still struggling. "Thank God, you came! I need your help," she said when she saw me. I demonstrated the technique to the students and then all of them came up with all kinds of questions. It was so evident that she has not been teaching them anything.'

I go to the bathroom, change my pants and come out. 'This is really, really terrible! Jabba keeps saying that she is the best teacher ever and this is what she is actually like? Before, she was able to manage things because I was doing all the teaching and she was just adding words here and there, like a background singer swaying and repeating the lyrics and there I was thinking we are a great team and are performing an awesome duet!'

'Yeah, that is terrible but don't get so worked up about it,' Nisha says as I sit down next to her.

'Don't get *worked up*? What do you mean by don't get worked up? What they are doing is outrageous! She is not fit to be a teacher. The only reason Jabba has appointed her is so he can keep . . . smooching her and . . . keep making love to her!'

'I know . . . but that is not *your* problem.'

'How is it *not* my problem?' I look at her.

'God! Calm down. And please stop yelling.'

'I am not yelling,' I say and realize that I actually am yelling. 'I am not yelling,' I repeat meekly. 'But it is my problem. I am a part of that institute and if I see anything wrong happening around me, it's my duty to do something about it.'

'Your duty is to teach the class that you have been assigned. *That* is your responsibility. And don't forget that it's Jabba who has appointed you. He is your boss. It won't do you any good to go against him. You tried doing that once and you know what happened. It won't be difficult for him to prove that you are not efficient at your job if you go against him or try to expose him.'

I know she is right and he has done that with me once in the past which puts me in an even more vulnerable position but I don't want to believe what she is saying.

'They are spoiling student's lives and careers,' I say squeaking like a mouse.

'Anyway, you tell me. How's your work going?' I change the topic to calm myself down.

'It's going fine,' Nisha sighs. 'Virath is coming to Delhi tomorrow. God, he has some money, man! He has a permanent suite at The Leela, you know.'

Huh! Of course he has a permanent suite at The Leela—that's where he molests and has sex with all those women he's constantly seen with, I scream in my head. Unfortunately, this thought is doing nothing to calm me down.

'Hmm . . . interesting . . .' I utter.

'He has asked me to come over for a discussion to his suite tomorrow evening.'

This is not right. I've got to tell her to stay away from him. Nothing good is going to come out of collaborating with him. He is only going to use her and then throw her away and not even work with her on the project later. Lightning flashes and deafeningly loud thunder roars outside. I turn and look outside the window. The cloud cover is thick as ever and it's still raining like crazy; it just does not seem like the storm is going to end. I gather all my courage, take a deep breath, face her and finally say it, 'Nisha, I don't think working with Virath is a good idea.' One of us has to take the step for the betterment of the relationship to secure it and make it stable.

She looks at me with an expression that I find hard to meet. It is like there is fire in her eyes and her jaw is clenched tight.

After a few seconds of silence, she finally speaks up, 'And why is that?' looking at me with very hard and angry eyes.

She is furious but it's good that we are having this

conversation—it's very important to confront matters rather than hide them.

'Because that guy, Virath, he is a pervert. He has asked you to join him at his . . . grand, luxurious and . . . expensive suite only because he . . . wants to make out with you. He wants to sleep with you.'

Her face is serious as she asks, 'And what makes you think that I am going to go ahead with it or that I am incapable of handling him?'

'It's not about being able to handle him or not. It's just . . . *why* do you want to get involved with all this? You know what's going to happen? The media is going to be all over this and then they'll start with all the gossip . . . why do you want to get into all that?'

'More than me not being able to handle it, I think it's you who is having trouble handling the situation.' She has her arms crossed across her chest now. This is her no-nonsense look; she always has it when she is irritated.

'Come on, Nisha, we both know what kind of a man he is.'

'You know, Rohit, for someone who was caught watching a porn video just last week, you have some nerve to say all this!'

Uff! She's never going to let go of that, is she?

She carries on, 'Besides, in our careers, Rohit, we are going to come across all kinds of people. We have to make choices and see what is going take us forward.'

'Yes, but—'

'And don't tell me that you don't come across crazy fans who send you inappropriate mails.'

Oh my God! Let it go, woman!

'Yes, but that is different. I never meet them . . .'

She lets out a little laugh, 'This is *so* typical. Anything you do, anything you decide is all right, it's *all* justified. But whatever I do has to be put under the microscope.'

'Not everything. I am just talking about this one thing.'

The silence seems to stretch for hours. Until, finally, Nisha breaks it. 'Rohit, I think I have made up my mind. I don't think this relationship is going anywhere. I think it's regressive for both of us. There is no point in staying together any more.'

'What do you mean?! No. *No!* I was just telling you—' I say with a sinking feeling.

'That's the problem, Rohit, you think you have to *tell* me everything. It's like taking dictation all the time!'

'That's not true. I ask you for suggestions too.'

'There is a difference in asking for suggestions and telling one what to do. I am sorry to learn that you don't know the difference.'

I look at her blankly. I don't know what to say. There is only an angry silence in the room that is being fed into an ugly monster by the sound of the heavy rain beating madly against the windowpanes shut tight so as not to let the slightest draught of wind inside.

'This whole relationship is suffocating me and my career, Rohit. I have actually been thinking about it for a while now. It's best for us to part ways.' She stands up and starts pacing. 'I will come tomorrow to take my stuff. I will leave my set of the keys to the apartment here.' She taps on the cabinet next to the door, picks up her car keys and walks out the door.

And I had started the conversation to improve and balance the relationship.

I sit in shock when I watch her standing in the doorway once again. 'And, for your information, I know about the regular sex chats you are having with that *fan* of yours.' And she storms out again.

I am at a loss. I don't know what to do. I am still frozen to the spot when Pranav comes in, 'What happened, sir-ji? I met Nisha ma'am outside the lift. Why was she so angry?'

I look at him in a daze. He is absolutely drenched from head to toe and water is still dripping from his hair.

'I don't know . . . I don't think I can explain right now.'

'Oh ho! You had a fight with her. Don't worry. It's not the first time. I've handled it before, I'll handle it again,' he says, ruffling his hair and spraying drops of water around.

I have nothing to say but I am extremely worried.

32

The ray of hope dies. No change in Rohit's life what-so-ever—Ravi Kapoor

His lifeless form turns cold as they wheel it out of the ICU on a stretcher. Ravi Kapoor breathed his last at 2.41 p.m. The media will splash this sensational news everywhere; within minutes it will be on TV and on the radio. Tomorrow's newspapers will carry a full-page spread about his life, his achievements and how grand and important a personality he was in Bollywood and how the void he's left behind can never be filled.

The rain continues to fall in sheets. It is an unnatural, unseasonal shower that is disturbing everyone's daily activities. Earsplitting roars of thunder and brilliant flashes of lightning rent the sky as Ravi Kapoor's wife puts final touches to her face, trying to get her skin tone just right for when she will be photographed by the media as the 'grieving wife of the emperor of romance' in Bollywood.

33

The winds of disappointment—Tara

The bleak ray of hope has vanished again. The tiny drop of happiness has evaporated before it could even reach her. She wanted to do this one last thing for the boy she had been in love with since she had understood the idea of love. She wanted to make it on her own, she wanted to get her book published without taking anyone's help. But that was impossible now. She had to take someone's help.

Tara picks up her purse and pulls out Rohit Sehdev's business card that Meetali's friend Nisha had given her and puts it on the table next to her laptop. She is going to mail him and ask him to help her get her published so that her love can live forever.

34

Some people think that we don't need to write anything new. So much has been written already. We only need to copy, paste and say that we wrote it—Karun

Facebook is the new Google, only better—you can promote and advertise your work for free. You just need to figure out which people to get in touch with and make them follow you. I have been doing a bit of a research lately and have come up with a wonderful plan. So many people are writing these days—everyone wants to become an author. In one respect, they are competition. But from another, if they all come together and help each other, it will be really positive for all of them. I have got a total of thirty-seven first-time authors in my friends' list. And this is the group message I am sending them.

```
Dear Friends,
    Let me introduce myself. My name is Karun
```

Mukharjee and I am the bestselling author of the hugely successful novel *My Love, My Angel is the Best Thing in My Life,* which is still creating waves after over a year of its release. I have been following you guys for some time now and I have seen that all of you have a good number of friends here on Facebook. If we all come together, form a group here on FB and add all the people in our friends' lists, then, according to my calculations, we will be able to reach over 50k people. I believe this a good figure to achieve without paying any kind of money for any FB ads—any post that we put up will directly reach more than 50k people. We can also promote each others' work and build our credibility among our readers. It's a 100 per cent foolproof plan—a win-win for each one of us. Let me know how many of you are in. I think we can really make our books sell here this way.

Best,

Karun

Yes, I know I am a genius—super-large-scale marketing for free. Now it's time for my daily FB update—copy a quote from bestquotesonline.com and share it on my timeline as something I have written. I know for a fact that no one ever gets to know it's not original—no one is that well-read these days!

35

He is completely miserable now; his life is totally empty without Nisha—Rohit

Respected Sir,

   We are doing a story about the young and upcoming authors and would like to interview you for the same. Please find the set of questions listed below and kindly send the answers as a reply to this mail. We will be grateful if you could send the answers by tomorrow evening before 4 p.m.

1. What made you consider writing as a career and switch your profession?
2. Your books have many references to popular movies, TV series and books. Any special reason for such choices?
3. All of us have reasons for what we do in our lives. Do you have any special reasons for writing?

4. We understand that you are a voracious reader—what are you reading these days?

5. Your books, unlike many of your contemporaries, do not have any 'sleazy' content, as you put it. Why?

6. There are so many young people out there who follow what many people call 'the paperback dreams' of today and aspire to become bestselling authors. Do you have any message for them?

Warm regards,

Bhavya Vishist,

For *Indian Times*

New Delhi

I blink at my computer screen and try to rack my brain for the answers to these questions but the brain is actually a very irritating entity—in emergency situations and moments of desperation, it always chokes and makes us panic. The more you try to make it think, the more it panics. There is no point in stressing over these questions. I will answer them later, peacefully, when I am a bit relaxed and . . . better. The journalist needs the answers by tomorrow evening and the story will be in the papers the day after. I have time to send the answers. It will be nice to see my name in the papers actually. It's been ages since I have seen any articles about me. In fact, the last time anyone wrote anything about me was when that One-Day-Lit-Fest-of-the-Year happened. It's been almost a year since then.

I shut down my laptop and walk out of my room. The living room looks gloomy. I go to the kitchen and put water to boil for tea. Why the hell did I fight with her? It was just this one stupid thing—I should have just let go of the pinch of her working with that pervert. I look around: the living room is a mess, hazily lit by the golden light of the morning sun and peppered with the soft long shadows of the furniture in the room. There are books and magazines littered everywhere. There are printouts of the typed manuscript that I am working on. My world is totally empty and incomplete without Nisha. My house was never a mess when she was around. *I* was not such a mess. I start collecting all the junk. What the hell is wrong with me? I have a career to take care of—I have a bloody novel to finish! The one thing I do not need is to think and cry over my ex-girlfriend who left me because she chose her career over trying to make me feel better about the way things were going. I gather the pages of my manuscript and flop on the couch. It's a funny feeling I get in my chest—heavy and light at the same time, an uneasy mix of emptiness and want. Why isn't she calling me? Is there no way we could work this out? Where is she right now? What is she doing? I look at the clock on the wall; it's 8 a.m. This is when she has her green tea every day. Is she drinking it today as well, with half a teaspoon of sugar and a dash of lemon? I want to talk to her. I want to know where she is, and what she is doing.

'Good morning, sir-ji.' Pranav comes out of his room with a lazy walk, rubbing his eyes.

'Morning,' I throw my head back and close my eyes.

After a minute or so I hear, 'Sir-ji, tea.'

I open my eyes as Pranav puts two cups of green tea on the table in front of me.

'Thank you,' I struggle to smile.

'Don't worry, sir-ji,' he pats me on the shoulder. 'Everything is going be all right.'

Despite his attempt to console me, something inside me says that this time is not going to be like the numerous times in the past when we have fought and then made up later. I had never seen Nisha the way she was when she left this time.

'I have not felt this terrible in ages.' I sigh. 'This is not how things are supposed to be. We were together for a reason; we were to be together for life. How could she just go away?' I shake my head. This is misery. This is sheer misery. 'My life sucks. My life sucks terribly. Everyone hates me. No one wants to be with me. Maybe I am *supposed* to be this miserable person who is destined to live a miserable life and just . . . rot! People always abandon me; no one ever stays with me.'

I want to break down. I want to cry my heart out and never stop.

'Hello! Sir-ji!' Pranav says waving his hands all over in the air, 'I am sitting right here; I am still here.'

I look at him; I look at him for a while as my eyes well up and get all shiny and I smile for a bit. I know that Pranav is here and is really fond of me and does care a lot. But for some reason, that is not enough. This will not fill the emptiness inside me. Things feel so painfully incomplete. I want Nisha back. I want to see her face again and play with her hair once more. I want to talk to her . . . hold her in my arms again. Only that, and nothing else, will make me happy.

36

When he does not get live sex, he switches to cyber sex—Jeet

'We cross-checked it twice, sir. We are a 100 per cent sure that it's Karun who has been writing all those hate mails and bad reviews.' I can't believe what the IT consultant at my PR agency is saying. 'We checked the IP address and then traced the location. It was Karun's residence.'

That son of a bitch! That fucking bastard!

'Thank you for your help, Raman. I am driving to office right now, can't talk for long. Please send me an invoice for your services for this month; I want to make the payment before the end of the month.'

'Sure, sir, I will do that. Thank you.'

'Thanks, bye.' I disconnect the call.

That kid is such a prick! I need to find a way to squash him out of my way. I pull into my spot in the parking lot and walk to the office. The day has started on such a terrible note.

I sit at my desk and turn on my computer. There are a

dozen new unread emails; I click open the one at the top of the inbox. It's this week's Tellson's Book Count India list. I quickly run through it and see that three of our titles are in the top twenty-five titles in the list. Running that controversy paid well after all. We should do this more often—post our sex videos on the Internet. But I don't know what is up with Neeti these days—she is just not up for sex. Something is bothering her. She has made it very evident that the media is not giving her enough recognition and appreciation but does that bother her so much?

A chat window opens on my Facebook page.

Saima: hello sexy

Who is this girl? I look closely at her display picture and she is rather cute.

Jeet: Hello
Saima: U are d God
Jeet: ?
Saima: d God of SEX
Jeet: LOL!
Saima: No, srsly. Ever since I've seen that video. . .
Jeet: LOL! . . .what?
Saima: just can't stop thinking of u
Jeet: ☺
Saima: Will u send me a pict of urslf?
Jeet: Sure. You can download whichever one you like from my Facebook account. I have left them free for download for everyone.

Saima: nt dose kind of picts ;)

Jeet: Sorry?

Saima: Wht r u wearing

Jeet: jeans and T-shirt. What are you wearing?

Saima: I m only in my panties

Jeet: nice

Saima: I want u to tk off all ur clthes, click a pic of urslf n send it to me

Jeet: LOL! I am in office.

Saima: pls ☹

Jeet: Okay. But one condition.

Saima: ?

Jeet: you have to send me your picture too, in just what you are wearing right now.

Saima: Deal. Bt no face

Jeet: no face either

So, my sex life is reduced to mere cyber sex now. But anyway, something is better than nothing. I bolt the door to my office. It's a good thing that Neeti is late for office again today. It's time for some virtual stimulation and one-sided action.

37

He may be in denial but the truth is that he can't get over Nisha—Rohit

I must do what all writers do—use all my energy, feelings, experiences and memories for my writing. I must channel the pain and agony of this excruciatingly hurtful break-up into the story I am writing, most realistically with all the true feelings that I have. My lead character is going to break up with his true love. I don't care if it fits in the story or not, it's what is going happen to him. I will find a way to break his relationship up with his *GF*! There is always space for break-ups in a story.

Raging thoughts whirl in my mind as I walk down the corridor to the faulty room. I have just finished delivering a lecture to the first years who just don't have their heads in the right place, I don't know why. All they want to do is challenge the teacher and question the syllabus. There is something seriously wrong with this generation, I tell you! They only want to come to college and make girlfriends and boyfriends and fool around with them. I have eavesdropped on them so many times—*I know the truth*. I know it's bad to eavesdrop on people, but I can't help it—it's my job to know what's happening around me—*it's my business to know their business*. How else am I supposed to write? And moreover, the students also eavesdrop on my conversations; they always want to know what we teachers are talking about. So it's only fair.

And talking about students wanting to fool around and have sex, just look at the couple at the end of the corridor. I can only see them in a silhouette but their wild desires are clearly visible even in this faint light. The boy is fat, like really fat. I wonder how many people he ate before he came here. The girl is crying and he is wiping her tears. God! I hate such drama! Now the fat boy is holding her face by her chin and saying something to her. He hugs her and they start to kiss. Okay, this is not done! I've got to put an end to this ridiculously ugly display of affection. I start striding towards them and as I near them I get the shock of my life! They are not a couple of students; they are Jabba the Hutt and Megha! Oh God! Oh God! I must retreat! I must go back and hide somewhere! I tiptoe backwards and turn away, hoping they haven't seen me, as they go on with their passionate kiss.

God! Things are way worse than I thought they were! I walk with my head down and do not look up till I'm inside the faculty room. In my cabin I quietly fiddle with all the papers piled there to distract myself and wash away the revolting image of the dean kissing Megha.

I pretend to be busy when I hear someone call, 'Sir?'

Ramona is standing in front of me. The look in her eyes tells me that something is terribly wrong.

'Hey, what happened?' I ask.

'All hell has broken loose, sir! And I really don't know what to do!' Her eyes are popping out. I have never seen her like this before.

'Today we had our art appreciation class,' she begins, 'with Megha ma'am. Like every day, she came and started writing on the board and asked us to take notes. Before the class began, Pranav and I were discussing how all Megha does is copy matter from the textbook and write it on the board instead of giving lectures and having discussions in the class. Pranav refused to write down anything that Megha scribbled on the board. I told Pranav not to do that as it would only piss Megha off but he didn't listen to me. When Megha saw he was not taking notes she asked him to stand up and asked him why. He said that he has the textbook and will go home and read it; he does not need to waste time noting down what she copies from the book and writes on the board. Megha got very angry and told him to shut up but he went on and on about how she did not know anything about teaching and should go and learn how to teach first and then come and teach us. This made her really mad; she started yelling like crazy and told him to get out of the class.

'Pranav refused. Instead, he opened his laptop and started writing a letter to the chancellor of the university to complain against her on behalf of our whole class. Megha had no idea what he was doing. She ignored him and started writing on the board again. After a while she turned to Pranav again and asked him to close his laptop and pay attention in class. By then he had sent the mail and was chatting on Facebook. He said he did not want to attend the rest of the lecture and walked out. Megha was furious! She started yelling, screaming that we were all 'evil sons of bitches' and our parents are shitty, they have not taught us any manners. Then she threw the marker on the floor, grabbed her things and stormed out of the class, crying. I think she went to the dean, sir. It's really serious; I hope the dean does not expel Pranav from college.'

This explains everything. This explains why Jabba was wiping tears off Megha's cheeks in the corridor.

I don't understand why Pranav has to be so aggressive all the time. He should have just excused himself on the pretext of going to the bathroom and not returned for the rest of the class. That is what I used to do for the classes that were conducted by terrible teachers.

'Don't worry,' I console Ramona, 'things are going be fine. Just send Pranav to me. Where is he?'

'I don't know where he is. I will just call him.' She pulls her out cell phone from her pocket and calls him as she walks out of the faculty room.

I fiddle with the papers in my cabin again, trying to figure out what I was doing before Ramona came when I hear an angry voice yell my name, 'Rohit!'

'Yes, sir.' I spring up from my seat. It's Jabba.

'I want to see you in my office right now!' he shouts angrily and stomps out.

God! What's with all the anger? I must go to his office right now. But I must talk to Pranav before that.

I flip out my phone and call him.

'Yes, sir-ji,' he takes my call.

'Pranav, go to Jabba's office and apologize *right now*!'

Nothing can be more urgent—this is an emergency!'

'But, sir-ji, it was not my fault . . . she does not know how to teach—'

'Shut up.' I cut him off. There is no time for any of this.

'Okay, sir-ji.' He sounds disheartened.

In less than a minute I am in Jabba's office. As soon as he sees me, he says, 'Call all the final year students. Call the whole class; I want to talk to them.'

'Yes, sir.' I nod.

Within moments all the students from the final year are standing in front of Jabba, in his office.

'Thieves! You are thieves!' he yells.

No one, including me, understands what he means but still no one dares to question him—no one wants to nudge him in this horrible avatar of his.

'Thieves! You are thieves! All of you are robbing your parents of their money. They have paid so that you come here and study and that is the last thing you do! Thieves! You are thieves!' he says, slamming his hands on the table just like a mad man who is having a fit or something.

I see some students trying to suppress their laughter. I don't blame them; he actually looks funny right now. He is so angry that he is almost bursting out of himself. His eyes are bloodshot and are popping out like boiled eggs and each time he slams his hands on the table, his fat belly is jiggling. Honestly, I am also trying to suppress my laughter.

'Hey you!' he suddenly yells. I instantly look at him! No, he has not seen me struggling to kill my laughter. He is pointing at a student who has rolled up the collar of her shirt so that he cannot see her laughing. 'You!' he yells again as he treads briskly towards her.

'Stop laughing,' he says as he shoves her violently and the girl loses her balance and falls down on the floor. God! He is crossing the line now! He is *so* crossing the line now. Some of the other students help the girl to her feet; she has tears in her eyes. Seriously, man, what is wrong with him? All this for a teacher who clearly cannot teach well and needs to gain more experience before she can be given the charge of building the careers of these students.

Pranav is also standing among the kids and the look on his face tells me that he did not like the way Jabba just behaved. God! I seriously hope he does not do something terrible here now. I don't want things to go worse right now.

'Sir.' Pranav speaks up. There is fire in his eyes.

Jabba looks at him.

'I am sorry.' He says, his eyes fixed on the fat man.

And then he looks at me. He does not say anything but I can almost hear him speak—*You asked me to, so I did. Otherwise I would never have apologized to this fat bastard.*

'Shut up! Shut up, you!' Jabba yells even louder as he almost runs to Pranav.

'You know what you are? You are a criminal. You should be stripped naked in public and whipped bloody! ALL OF YOU SHOULD BE STRIPPED NAKED AND WHIPPED BLOODY! ALL OF YOU ARE THIEVES! THIEVES! ALL OF YOU BELONG IN JAIL!'

What I want is for Jabba to have a heart attack and die *right now* but that does not happen.

Someone needs to handle the situation. Someone needs to put an end to this or it will go on forever.

'Sir,' I step forward. 'Please calm down, please.'

'NO I WILL NOT CALM DOWN! YOU DON'T KNOW THESE . . .' he holds his tongue to control his language—'. . . Imbeciles! THEY ARE IMBECILES!' he yells.

'Sir, they are young. They made a mistake. They are apologizing now. They won't repeat such a thing again.'

'Repeat?' he turns and looks at me with his head tilted to one side, 'Do you think not repeating a thing like this is all it takes? Can they undo the letter that has gone to the chancellor's office? NO ONE CAN!' he thunders again. 'You know, Megha has been crying like a baby since morning. I have not been able to make her stop.'

Liar. I saw him put his tongue in her mouth and make her stop crying. I look at the students standing silently with their heads bowed. The girl whom Jabba had just pushed is openly sobbing now, occasionally wiping away her tears. Jabba cares so much when it is Megha who's crying but is so insensitive to this girl who is hurt, both physically and emotionally.

'I can take care of the situation. I will make sure that no action is taken against her. The students were misbehaving in the class and that is the truth.'

'Sir, please calm down,' I repeat.

'We are sorry, sir.' Another student speaks up from the crowd.

'Come on, sir, forgive them.' I pat Jabba on the shoulder when what I really want is to punch him in the eye.

He remains silent for a few seconds, takes a deep breath.

'It's not their fault, sir; it was not their intention to get Megha in trouble. It was just something they did on the spur of the moment, without realizing what the consequences could be. Students at this age are like that sometimes.'

Jabba takes a deep breath and says, 'Okay, you guys can leave now. And you better mend your ways.'

Thank God! Thank God!!!

All the students start to file out of the office but Pranav turns to look at Jabba and Jabba glares back at him. Neither one of them says anything but it's as though I can hear their silent exchange.

—When I said 'sorry' I did not mean it, you fat bastard. No matter how many times you fuck Megha, you're not going make her a better teacher.

—This is not over yet. I have not forgiven you, Pranav. I am going teach you a lesson.

38

Who needs old friends when they are of no use anymore?—Karun

I have always believed that in order to be certified as a celebrity, you've got to have a popular sex scandal under your belt, along with your active goodies. And what I see has reinforced my belief even more. I stare at the screen of my phone, unsure of whether I am in awe of the sheer genius of Jeet Obiroi or if I am jealous that I did not get this idea before he did. It really is a steaming hot video. I am actually getting a boner from watching it while I wait for Vishal in this coffee shop to discuss our next plan of action. This Neeti girl has a super hot body, I mean look at her breasts, man! Now that the world has seen them naked, everyone is going want to read their book to know what they write. Their plan has worked perfectly; just look at the number of views this video has had—1,48,320! And this video is just two days old, mind that. I need to do something, man! I need to create a sex scandal of my own quickly. I would have done this same thing if Devika were here. Maybe I can make a sex video of myself. Yes, I should totally do that. I will put up a video of myself jerking off without showing my face and then fuel this rumour that it's me. All I need to do is make a fake profile and post that video on the authors' group I have created with the title *See the bestselling author Karun Mukharjee fapping* and that's it.

'Karun?'

God! Now who the fuck is that? I turn around and see Ishan.

'How are you, man?' he walks to me as if he wants to come and hug me, as if he has seen a long-lost friend after ages. True, we go to the same school but I don't understand his new-found affection for me. Maybe he is behaving like this because I have become so famous now. After the success of my book, I am *the* guy everyone talks about in school.

'I am good.' I am in no mood to stand up and greet him. I am in the middle of something here.

'Where *are* you, man! I have not seen you in *ages*! You don't even answer my calls.'

Seriously? What makes him think I'll take his calls? Does he ever have anything meaningful and important to say? I don't say anything, all I can do is smile awkwardly and look at him.

'What's up, man? Don't you have any time for your friends? We are worried about you.' He blinks back at me.

'Nothing much. Just work—this and that. And please! Stop behaving like you are my girlfriend.' There is no point explaining what's up these days—he won't understand anything.

He just stands there. 'You have changed, man, you are not the same Karun any more.'

What the fuck is his problem? Why won't he just go away?

'You are so consumed with your fame and success that you can't see anything else around you; you can't even see the things you are losing, the things you have already lost. I have not seen you in school in days.'

What the fuck is this asshole's problem? How do I get rid of him? Just then I see Vishal walking towards me. I get up to greet him and we shake hands.

'Hi, how are you? Please sit.' I offer.

'I am good, how are you?' Vishal asks.

'Great,' I say. There is an awkward silence for a moment as Ishan hovers for a while. Finally, he speaks up, 'I think you are busy. I'll just leave.'

'Yeah, see you later.' I wave at him as he walks away. Fucking moron. 'So, Vishal, tell me. How are things shaping up?'

'I have done everything as you asked me to. I have talked to the organizers of the One-Day-Lit-Fest-of-the-Year and have arranged for you to be on the same panel as Rohit. I am also ready with all the battery of questions you asked me to throw at Rohit during the event.'

'This is brilliant! Being on the same panel as Rohit is going make things so easy for me. And with the book that he had written already out under another author's name, it is going be so much fun.' I laugh.

'You are so wicked, man.'

'And so are you, otherwise why would you ever partner with me in this crime.'

Vishal looks back at me and smiles.

'There's one more thing I wanted to ask you. These Popular

Book Awards . . . I want to win them this year. Do you have any idea how we can lobby for it?'

He looks at me for a while, 'You are one hungry beast, aren't you?'

I smile back at him, 'Everyone wants to be famous; everyone is hungry like that. The only difference is that some have the guts to make it happen and some don't.'

'I can push your book up to the point of being shortlisted for the award. But I won't be able to help you beyond that.'

'That'll be great. If that book reaches that level, I am sure it will win because all the other books that are out in the market right now are pig shit compared to it.'

Vishal nods.

'Here is the next instalment for your payment.' I put the blank envelope with the money on the table. 'And I have a few more requests for you this time.'

'As always, you want a little extra this time too.' He smiles.

'Along with Rohit, I want you to put a few bad words about Ject Obiroi also. And in your next article, I also want you to write that Karun Mukharjee and Neeti are co-authoring a book that will release early next year.'

39

**It's sad to know at times who gets the last laugh
—Rohit**

Shitty things happen in life all the time. But that does not mean that we stop paying attention to the wonderful things that happen to us (once in a while). It's not every day that the things I say are published in a newspaper. It's been a week since I sent the answers to the questions Bhavya Vishist sent me from the *Indian Times*. I wonder if they'll put a picture of me in the newspaper too, I am not sure if I want that—I never look good in my pictures. Maybe this interview will give a boost to my career. Maybe this interview will lead to other interviews and people will like them so much that they'll all read my books and tell everyone they know what a great writer I am! I could become the bestselling author in India! And all of this is happening at just the right time.

My next book, my most ambitious project ever, should be releasing by the end of this year. This is the time when I should start catching people's attention. I am so confident about my next book that it's not even funny. I mean who does not want to know how the highest selling author of India came into existence—what's his story? Anyway, right now I need to read my interview in the paper. It's a pity that I don't subscribe to *Indian Times*. I need to go out and get a copy from the bookshop in the market next to my apartment building.

I peep into Pranav's room and he is still sleeping. It's 9 a.m., but I don't blame him—he had a tough day yesterday. I decide to lock the door from the outside; I'll be back in less than ten minutes.

The man behind the counter at the bookstore is sitting next to a stack of neatly arranged 'new arrivals'.

'Do we have today's *Indian Times*?' I ask him.

Without looking at me, the guy nods and pulls out a copy of the newspaper from the newspapers spread out on the table next to him while I flip through the new arrivals. There is nothing that really interests me; it's just a pile of the usual stuff. I pay for the newspaper and am about to leave when my eyes fall on a book. I freeze. I cannot believe my eyes. My heart sinks; I cannot feel the ground beneath my feet. What the hell is this? How can this be? I pick up the book and stare at it. I am not hallucinating. *Paperback Raja*, the title of the reads. I run my hand over it in disbelief. This cannot be . . . this *just cannot be*! The book has been published by my old publisher, Dash Publishers; the name of the author is Rubin Sharma. I have no clue who he is. I turn it over to read the blurb and there is a picture of him. Narrow slits for eyes and all his teeth visible like a chimp. *I hate him!*

David Behel is an IIT-D IIM-B graduate for whom money is not everything. He wants fame and will get it at any price. Follow his story from the days of his college to the time when be becomes the undisputed king of the new genre that he creates and becomes the bestselling Indian author in English of all time.

I quickly read through a few pages of the book and want to rip it to shreds; I want to pour acid on it and destroy it! It's the same story I finished writing last month and sent to that editing service I hired: We are for the Writers. This is totally insane! This can't be true! It's one of those terrible nightmares that only happen to people in the movies.

I walk back to my apartment in a daze. My whole world has ended. I am finished. My writing career is over. I have got nothing to live for now. My biggest and most ambitious project ever has been stolen and published before I even sent it to my publisher! I want to weep. I want to burn the whole world, including that book, its author and my old publisher who brought this whole sinister plan to life. How could they do this to me? And *why* would they do this to me? Is this his way of taking revenge for what I did to him at the Lit Fest last year?

When I enter the apartment, a sleepy-eyed Pranav is standing in the doorway of his room.

'Sir-ji, what happened?' he asks, shocked.

'Nothing,' I sigh bitterly, 'except my whole writing career just crashed to an end and died.'

How I wish that Nisha was here. Problems never seemed big when she used to be around.

40

**Othello lives on—misunderstandings do end things
even today—Jeet**

This girl is smoking hot! And she has become my everyday
habit—my morning dose of sex. It's funny how we don't know
much about each other but can still arouse each other so easily
even through an indirect medium like the Internet. I quickly
finish my business after Saima sends me a new picture of her
'real' self and zip up my jeans.

I quickly log off from Facebook for the morning, walk to
the main door to fetch today's newspaper and lay it down on
the table. Quickly, I glance at the headlines when something
catches my attention.

KARUN MUKHARJEE TO CO-AUTHOR HIS NEXT BOOK WITH
BESTSELLING NOVELIST, NEETI

Dedication and hard work always pay. Karun Mukharjee
is the perfect example of that truth. In less than a year this
young author has become the hottest selling author these days.

While his first book is still topping the charts, he has already announced this next book. Talking about his next book, the young author said, 'I can't tell you much about the book yet but I am just going say that it's going be a very sensational one. It will be a story about an author who gets a book written by someone else under his own name. The character I am developing is very interesting; he can't live without the fame he has gained. I will be co-authoring this book with Neeti. We have already started working on the story and hope to finish the story within the next three months.'

One cannot deny that the subject this author talks about does sound interesting.

I hear the main door open. It's Neeti. The clock on the wall says 11 a.m. She has been this late every single day for the past over two weeks. No wonder—it's because she's been meeting this Karun Mukharjee to work on her new book.

'Morning', she says as she flings her bag on the table next to her desk and sits down.

I do not reply. The fucking bitch!

There is an awkward silence in the room and she turns back to look at me.

'What happened?'

I pick up the newspaper and slam it in front of her. 'Did you really think I would never find out?'

'What?' she frowns at me and then looks at the paper. 'This is bullshit!' she bursts out after quickly reading the article.

'Oh come on! Stop lying. It's all out now.'

'No, Jeet, this is—'

'Please, Neeti, stop this act now. You've been coming to office late every day . . . you aren't even interested in writing our next book any more—'

'No, Jeet—'

'Now I understand everything. You teamed up; you teamed up with that sneaky little bastard to write all those hate mails and bad reviews. You are despicable, Neeti, you are despicable. I gave you everything; I made you who you are today,' I say, shaking my head. God! She is such a lying bitch! 'You were a struggling nobody! I should have left you where you were. I should never have helped you. I should never have responded to your sad, flirtatious and desperate attempt to talk to me during that train journey. "I am getting married," you said! And what did you tell him, huh? What did you tell him about me and my life?'

'Jeet!' she yells.

'You are a selfish, self-centred . . . parasitic . . . manipulative . . . bitch!'

'JEET!' she fairly screams. 'You have no right to talk to me like this!'

'SHUT UP!' I thunder.

'YOU SHUT UP!' she roars back.

How dare she? How dare she talk to me like this in *my* office?

'Get out! Get out of my office, you scheming bitch.'

'I don't know what you are talking about.' She says as she picks up her bag. 'You are a selfish, fucking moron who cannot see anything beyond himself. You fucking bastard!' She falls silent and looks down at the floor and shakes her head. 'I am sorry, I am so sorry that I ever worked with you. I never regret a thing, but this is something that I am always going to regret in my life—knowing you—working with you. I did all the writing, I did all the hard work and all you ever did was bask in the glory of the book that *I wrote*. And this is how you repay me? You are pathetic, Jeet Obiroi, you are the most pathetic sick dog I have ever come across.'

I look into her eyes, trying to control my anger and rein in the urge to hit her. 'Shut up and get out of here. Go fuck this new sex buddy of yours and get the hell out of my office.'

She slings her bag on her shoulder, walks to the door, halts, turns and looks at me. 'You know something,' she nods her head, 'this day, it's the end of everything.' She gestures around the office, 'All this, this comes to an end today.' Her eyes are welling up but I don't see any sadness; I see only infinite anger that she is holding back. '*This* is the end of your career as an author because you will never be able to write again.'

She storms out of my office.

41

He is still completely clueless about what to do
—Rohit

What am I supposed to do now? How am I supposed to carry on? I have got no direction! All my months of hard work have just been snatched away from me in an instant! I am sitting on my bed and staring at the copy of the book that has destroyed my life. I lack the courage to open and read it. This whole thing, it's so brutal, it's so. . . cruel! I should have lived my life differently. I should have had a different set of values. I should not have rested my *whole* life on my work. I should have lived like other normal people and given more importance to relationships and stuff. God! Who am I kidding? That would not have been any good either. How can I forget that my girlfriend broke up and walked out on me just a few weeks back? My relationships suck too. I want to vanish! I want to sink in the ground and disappear. *This is miserable!*

'Sir-ji?' I hear Pranav call from from his room.

Oh God! No, not him again! He is going to start about

how I should get over this whole thing and move on. I don't understand him really. Doesn't he get it that I don't want to do anything right now? I want to just be in my pyjamas, let my beard grow, not shower for days and just . . . stay this way. I just can't take my mind off this terrible situation and I don't even want to. What use it will be? Someone out there wants me finished. Whatever I do, they are going make sure that it ends miserably. God! This is really hopeless.

'Sir-ji—' Pranav appears at the door.

'What is it?' I snap at him. He can be really irritating at times.

'Sir-ji, I need help. I can't get the strokes right for my painting. And I am not sure about the colour palette either.' He stands there scratching his head as he makes a face.

So this is his new trick—this is how he plans to get me out of my present state of mind. I am so not amused.

'Pranav, I saw the painting you were working on last night. It's coming out fine. The colours are fine and there is nothing wrong with the strokes either.'

'Sir-ji, *please*! Come and see it once,' he whines.

Someone please stop him. I look back into his eyes and flatly say, 'Pranav, I know what you are trying to do and it's not going work.'

Silence.

'My life is over . . . and there is nothing anyone can do to make it better,' I stammer.

'Oh my God!' Pranav jumps.

'God! What now?' I roll my eyes.

'I am calling the police!'

'For heaven's sake!'

'You are not Rohit sir! You are someone else! You are an *imposter*!'

'What the hell is *wrong* with you?'

'You are an imposter; you are not my Rohit sir. You have kidnapped my sir-ji and have hidden him somewhere.'

'Shut up.'

'My sir-ji is a very positive person; he would never talk or behave the way you are doing. I am calling the police.' He actually pulls out the phone from his pocket and starts to dial a number.

'Sir-ji, if you aren't up by the count of three, I am going to call the police and you can deal with them.'

Oh God, he is actually serious.

'Fine,' I grumble and get out of bed. 'What do you want me to do?'

'I want you to have breakfast first of all.'

'Okay.' I follow him out of the room.

'Now sit here.' He holds me by the shoulders and makes me sit on the sofa. 'I will get you your morning tea.'

Morning tea . . . breakfast. It used to be such a pleasant part of the day once upon a time. We were like a tiny family—Nisha, Pranav and me. And now there's nothing left. I stare at the floor as sad thoughts crowd my mind, drawing me into the past.

In a few seconds, Pranav comes out from the kitchen and puts a cup of tea on the table in front of me.

'God! Look at you,' he starts again.

Why doesn't he understand that I don't want to listen to a pep talk? I am not in the state of mind for one. Nobody can understand what I am going through, least of all him. How

can he? This is about my work and work is the last thing that
he has ever thought of.

'Okay, just one minute.' He turns around, marches into my
room and emerges moments later with that horrible, terrifying
book in his hands. He puts it in front of me on the table.

'This book is the reason for your misery, right?'

I nod. I am so upset I could cry. I had such great plans for
my story. With this story I was going make it big. This book
was going to be my gateway to success. And now it's gone, all
gone. I find it difficult to hold back my tears.

'Just tell me what you want to do with this book? This book
that has made you feel so terrible.'

Silence.

'Come on, sir-ji! Let it out! Get *rid* of it! *Express it!*' He
speaks as if he wants to hypnotize me.

I look at the book and feel anger rising like lava inside me.

'I want to destroy it,' the words come out harshly.

He picks up the book by a corner of the cover and gives it
a jerk. 'Oops!' he pretentiously exclaims as a part of the cover
remains in between his thumb and his forefinger while the rest
of the book crashes to the table. That he picks up the tea cup
he had got for me and splashes tea on the book.

'Oh no! I spilled tea on the book. Oh no! It was an
accident . . . completely unintentional!' He looks at me
wide-eyed as if he actually didn't mean to spill the tea. Such
overacting he does. He is such a clown.

'See, you are smiling now. I told you, you just needed to
do *bad things* to this book. What do you want to happen to
this book next?'

'I want to see this book fly,' I say as if I am little Robin Arryn from *Game of Thrones*. I need to take a break from these books, I have been reading too many of them lately.

'That is no problem at all.' He picks the book and flings it out of the window. Then he turns to me, 'Anything else?'

'I want it to be run over by a car.'

'That can be arranged.' He grabs my wrist and pulls me along as he walks out of the apartment, snatching the car keys on his way.

In less than a minute we are out by my car. Pranav picks up the book from where it had landed when he chucked it out of the window and throws it in front of the car.

'Just stand here and watch,' he says, starting the car. He drives the car over the book, reverses, runs over it once more, drives forward, runs over it again, backs over the book again and finally kills the engine. Stepping out of the car, he picks up the book and walks over to me.

'God! This book looks so terrible now!' he laughs.

I can't help but laugh either—this is the craziest thing I have ever seen anyone do, ever.

'Is this enough or do you want more bad things to happen to this book?' Pranav looks at me.

'Just one thing.' I say and take the book from his hands. Walking over to the main gate of our housing society, I hurl the book away and watch as it goes flying in the air and then lands on the road where it is repeatedly run over by the many speeding vehicles.

'That's it,' Pranav says, putting his hand on my shoulder, 'now everything's going be fine.'

42

If you can't win an award, buy one—Karun

I think my plan has worked okay. Thirty-three out of the thirty-seven authors I had approached have replied positively. The total reach that I had calculated will go down a little but that won't be significant enough to worry about. Now I just need to send a quick 'message of motivation' to all the new bitches who have responded.

```
My dear friends,
    I welcome you all to this group which is
your sure short gateway to fame and success.
I have been observing the current literary
scene in India very closely and I feel that
to become anything in today's literary scene,
it's very important to win an award. I have
been thinking about it for a while now and
have come up with the perfect solution. We
should form an association without revealing
```

our identities and launch literary awards. We shall have representatives so that no one will know that we run and decide the awardees. We decide the categories for these awards in such a way that each of us gets an award. I think we should decide a name for this institution and get ourselves registered ASAP.

Best,

Karun

43

The way to happiness can be found by helping others, says Nisha—Rohit

I don't think I have any purpose in life left any more. Maybe I should kill myself and just stop living. But then they say that the beings that don't have a reason for their existence perish eventually. So maybe I don't need to kill myself, the cosmos itself will kill me. Or maybe I have already ceased to exist in this world (as a person)—all I do is lie on my bed like a log, getting up only to pee, poop or eat.

It's the most unbearable feeling of emptiness. All I want (most desperately) is somehow for things to fall back into place as they were. I want my career back. I WANT NISHA BACK! I want her to be with me, on my bed next to me. Had she been here, she would have never let me feel this way. She knew how to make me feel better. But she is not here, because she does not care about me.

I HATE HER!

They say heartache is the greatest pain one can experience.

Strangely, I don't feel any pain right now. Pain is what you feel when a blade slashes your skin and tears your muscles. Or when burning wood or hot metal touches your skin. But the presence of people who love you can help you feel better and forget that pain. This bloody heartache, however, is an infinite and constant feeling of anxiety and restlessness that can be ended only by the comforting and loving presence of the one you miss—the one you love. Which in my case can never be, so I think I am going dwell in this terrible state of misery forever, go mad soon and end up in a mental asylum in white robes, chained to my bed, foaming like a mad dog.

I toss to the other side on my bed. I want to cry!

'Sir-ji?'

It's Pranav in my room. Oh my God! He is going to try to pull me out of bed with another pep talk. I immediately close my eyes and pretend to be in a deep, unshakable sleep.

'Sir-ji? Uffo sir-ji, you are sleeping again. Get up, *please*!'

I keep up the pretence of being asleep.

'SIR-JI!' he yells at the top of his lungs.

'What?' I get up, rubbing my eyes.

'What, sir-ji? You are always sleeping.'

'What are you saying? I never sleep,' I say meekly.

'Please, sir-ji. It's six in the evening. This is no time to sleep.'

I don't say anything, I just sit there like a dud—he's right, this is not the time to sleep. I look outside the window where the sun is setting, making the thin clouds in the sky shine golden for one last time before darkness falls.

'Come on, sir-ji, let's go out and have momos. It's been such a long time since we did that.'

'Please, Pranav, I don't wanna go.' I am feeling so terrible I hope my eyes don't well up.

He looks at me for a bit and then comes and sits next to me on the bed, 'Sir-ji, please don't do this to yourself. It's okay. I also went through a break-up when I was in the seventh standard. I had thought my life was over, that I had nothing to live for. I even stopped studying and failed in the exams. Things became really terrible. My dad said there was no use sending me to school and I should start going to the factory with him. And that was when it struck me—if my dad took me out of the school and I went to the factory with him every day then I would never have another chance to make another girlfriend. So that very day I started studying hard, day and night, and passed my next set of exams. Everything was fine after that.'

The way he narrates his story is actually funny and I have to suppress my smile as I must keep looking serious and depressed, but he looks at me from the corner of his eye and catches my expression.

'Come no, sir-ji! Let's go!' he whines.

'No, I can't,' I say blankly.

'Why?'

I fumble in my mind for an excuse. As I look around the room I see my laptop lying uselessly in a corner next to the wall. 'I have to check my mail. I have not checked my mail for over a week now.' And that is actually not a lie. I pick up my laptop and hold it against my chest as though it is a shield which will protect me from the things I don't want to do.

'Sir-ji, you are very bad.' Pranav stamps his foot like a four year old and walks out of the room.

There are some twenty-odd unread mails but most of them are stupid promotional mails and useless forwards that I never even open to read. There are only three mails that are of any importance. One is from the organizers of the One-Day-Lit-Fest-of-the-Year who are inviting me to a panel discussion about the rise in crimes against women in India and the impact of the entertainment media on it. They want me to discuss the issue with none other than Karun Mukharjee. I almost laugh when I read the invite. They are out of their minds if they think that I will be a part of the discussion. There is no way I am ever talking to that super villain after the things he said to me at that party. But if I don't attend, people, including Karun, will think I am a coward. Besides it is a subject that interests me a lot. I have thought a lot about it and would love to talk about it.

I decide to give the invite some thought before sending my response.

The second mail is from a girl named Tara. Maybe it's fan mail from one of my few readers who still exist and have not forgotten me. Maybe someone wants to know if I am still alive or not.

I open the email.

```
Dear Sir,

    I got your email address from your friend
Nisha ma'am. She has been very kind to me
and has helped me a lot through the toughest
time of my life.
```

```
    Sir, I have written a novel based on
my experiences in life and I want to get
it published but I have failed to find a
publisher so far. Nisha ma'am told me once
that you might be able to help me find a
publisher. I would be extremely thankful if
you could help me or give me some direction
on this matter. I am sending the manuscript
of my novel as an attachment with this email.
    Regards,
    Tara
```

I stare at the screen for a while, trying to understand how I feel. This is the same girl Nisha had told me about once and wished she could help. Perhaps I can help her. It's what Nisha always wanted me to do. And if I do so, if I help Tara find a publisher, will I be able to win Nisha back? Will she come back in my life again? This is brilliant! This is the best plan of action ever! I am about to mail my publisher and forward Tara's manuscript to them when I remember that the third unread mail was from my publisher.

```
Dear Rahul,

    I hope you are doing fine and everything
is going great at your end.

    Our marketing team was on their field
survey yesterday when they came across a
book with a title and storyline similar to
the book you're writing. We discussed the
```

```
matter internally and came to the conclusion
that it would be best to hold the project
for now. Pushing another book in the market
with a similar story (even if we change the
title) is not a good idea for it will affect
the sales figures of the book and also make
the book seem unoriginal.
   We trust you understand the situation and
hope for your cooperation.
   Best wishes,
   Wishvish Bhomba
   For Big Publisher X
```

Are they kidding me? This is insane! I can't believe what I have just read! What the hell do they want me to understand? Instead of preparing a law suit to sue the people who stole my idea, they want to pull my book back and expect me to *understand*? This is outrageous! I am not even going reply to this mail.

I feel so irritated that I begin to feel suffocated in my cluttered, dingy room. I have to get out of here. As soon as I enter the living room, Pranav asks me, 'What happened, sir-ji?'

Should I tell him what my publisher has decided? Maybe I should keep the information to myself for a while and think about my next step. Perhaps I should sue my publisher for not taking action against the people who stole my story.

'The One-Day-Lit-Fest people want me to host a session with Karun.'

He looks at me thoughtfully and then says, utterly sincerely, 'Sir-ji, I think you should go.'

He is an idiot, a kid, what does he know?

'Sir-ji, you should go so that you can show them that you are a strong person who is not affected by Karun's childish attempts to trouble you. You should use this chance, this platform that they are offering you, to showcase yourself and your work and gain some popularity. Moreover, if you go, it will be a tight slap on Karun's face, telling him that none of his vile plans against you are ever going work.'

I look at him silently for a while and think. He's not that much of an idiot. What he is saying does make sense. I should actually go out there and show the world that I am a strong person. And I should not give up the idea of completing my book and getting it out to the public either. It's not that old, desperate world any more. The publishing world is not solely in the hands of the big publishers now. I can self-publish this story as an ebook and sell it online. Or maybe I could just make this book available for free download on the Internet. That could result in an unimaginable circulation of this book and it might become super popular in no time! I won't get any money out of it but the book will become a bestseller like none other. This is brilliant! I should totally do this!

44

And someone wants to meet him now—Karun

```
Karun,
    I read the newspaper article which stated
that we are working on a book together. Why
did you make this announcement? I want you
to meet me and explain this.
    Neeti
```

I can't help smiling. She wants to meet me. I know she is going to want to join hands with me—she is left with no other choice. She is a career-conscious girl; she'll never give up all that she has gained. My plan is finally going to bear fruit! It's time to celebrate.

45

He will push the limits to get what he wants now
—Rohit

This is not done! I just read the reply that I got from my publisher about Tara's manuscript and there is no way that I am going let them reject it like that. I read the manuscript myself and it is really beautifully written. I cried thrice while reading it—it is that touching! I am going to drive down to my publisher's office and am going to ask them in person why they're not accepting this manuscript. How can any publisher ever refuse to publish it? For once I am trying to help someone selflessly and I won't let *anyone* stop me! My career might be taking a nosedive right now but I swear I am going to help Tara. She has gone through hell and I know that.

I asked Pranav to get me all the information about Tarun. He was a masters of fine arts student at the college where I teach and had become very friendly with Jabba. Unfortunately, Tarun attended several parties at Jabba's place where he picked up many addictions. Those addictions spun out of hand and he died of a drug overdose. Jabba needs to be kicked out of the college but that is something I am going to take care of later. Right now, I am going to help Tara live her dream even if I tank my career. This is how I am going to keep my love for Nisha alive. I know that my love for her was always true and she only misunderstood me.

46

Winds of change—Tara

The world is cruel. If it was not so, then why would Tarun have died? She's convinced that her manuscript is never going to get published. Certain things are not meant to be. And you can never force anything into existence. Perhaps the purpose of writing her story was not to get it published but to help her break out of her misery and see the sun once again.

She is sitting on her bed with her laptop. This is her daily ritual after the short nap she takes when she reaches home from college—a quick run through on Facebook and then a check on her email. There is a new mail in her inbox today. It is a response from one of the publishers she had mailed her book proposal to. Another rejection, she thinks to herself. She is in no mood to read another rejection letter, the ones that read as if lifeless metal robots have written them. Maybe she should just delete the mail without reading it, but she decides otherwise.

Thank God!

Dear Tara,

We read your manuscript and we found it very interesting. We would love to publish your story. We are making an offer for the manuscript. Please read the attached document for the details of the offer.

Best,

Wishvish Bhomba

For Big Publisher X

47

That angry, fiery stage fight—Rohit

Many hands rise up as the girl sits and one of the volunteers for the festival runs to another girl who wants to ask me a question.

'Good morning, sir. My name is Subalaxmi and I am a huge, huge fan.'

'Thank you.' I smile.

'First of all, let me thank you for being a part of this event and giving us all a chance to listen to your wonderful thoughts.'

'Thank you so much, Subalaxmi.'

I am sitting on the stage for the One-Day-Lit-Fest-of-the-Year once again. Maybe accepting their invitation was not that bad an idea after all.

'Sir, I have read both your books and I really love them.' She has a wonderful voice. 'Sir, in the fast-paced lives of today,' she continues, 'when we have to stay apart from our families for our studies or work, when we have such few true friends, if any, and our lives are so dry because we don't have many people or reasons to make us feel good, to make us smile, *you* are one of the people who give us this reason to smile. Your books have a feel-good factor and many wonderful moments that have made me smile. Thank you so much, sir.'

'Thank you.' I smile as my chin starts to wobble. I am so overwhelmed.

'And, sir, your writing has a very sweet innocence to it. Please don't ever lose it. Thank you so much for giving me a chance to speak,' she says as she sits down.

I smile, nod and gulp. This is the best thing anyone has ever said to me. This is like the greatest award I could have ever got. What she has just said actually sums up many of my reasons to write. Her kind words have left me so satisfied that even if I never get published again, I won't feel unsettled.

'And on that wonderful note, let's start our discussion for this session.' Svetlana, the beautiful blue-eyed presenter, who hosts this festival every year, speaks into the mic. I can clearly remember everything that happened last year as if it was yesterday. Today I am actually sitting on the platform that I had seen from a distance last year. Things are actually moving positively, it's just that I was never able to see that.

'We have gathered here to talk about a major problem in this country right now. We will be in conversation with two wonderful young authors: Rohit Sehdev and Karun Mukharjee who are here with us today. But before that we are just going talk to our guests about their interests.

Svetlana looks at me and smiles. 'I have a question for both of you. *Game of Thrones* from *A Song of Ice and Fire* has become the biggest phenomenon of our age and both of you have mentioned time and again that you are huge fans. Yet, as one can figure out from your work, you're both very different people. Then what makes you like the same things?'

I think for a moment about why I am such a crazy fan of the books and say, 'I like the books because they shake my emotions like nothing else. The story makes me hate and love those characters, and I haven't felt like that for any fictional characters in a long time.' I pause and think for a moment, 'And they are such endless books that one can keep on reading and still not fear that they are going end soon and then you will be left with a feeling of vacuum, having no more books of the kind to read.' What else? What else is it that I like about the books? 'And the detail in which those books are written almost makes you feel that you are reading actual history, not fiction,' I conclude.

'Very interesting.' Svetlana smiles and before she can ask Karun what he thinks, he speaks up by himself, 'My reasons go a bit deeper.' He gives me a look of pure hate. 'I like the books because they give me a deeper understanding of human psychology and help me deal with the world in a smarter way.'

'As they say, we all learn from what we read,' Svetlana chimes in. 'Rohit, I read in one of your interviews that you think that books are man's best companions. Now that's a very popular belief but I would like to know why you think so.'

'Because people never last. They either break your trust and betray you or leave you and go away.' I say this before I even realize what I am saying. I am struck with overwhelming emotions again as the memories of all the countless and wonderful mornings I spent with Nisha flood my mind. Waking up with her in my arms under those white bedsheets, lying in bed, feeling the warmth of her body and inhaling her scent as the golden rays of the morning sun filtered in through the window . . . wanting those moments to last forever. I must not let my eyes well up! I must not cry like a fool sitting here up in this stage. That will be totally ridiculous and get me very bad PR and media reaction.

Svetlana is about to open her mouth to say something when Karun jumps in like a baboon and says, 'But don't you think a person will leave someone if they have a problem with him? Don't you think in such cases a bit of retrospection is a good idea?'

I want to punch him in the eye!

'Of course. You are totally right.' I pretend a smile.

'Very well,' Svetlana says, looking at both of us a little awkwardly. 'Let us start with the main topic of discussion for our session.' She looks at the huge audience sitting in front of us and says, 'In the past one year, we have seen some of the most brutal and inhuman crimes against women. Today we are going discuss what we, as citizens of India, can do about it.' She turns to look at me, 'Rohit, what do you think about this problem?'

I have got it all prepared. 'The root of this problem, I think, is the fact that India is still majorly a patriarchal society. In most parts of the country, men marry women only because they need someone to sleep with. They don't have even the slightest mental or emotional connection with them. They consider them as objects, just like a piece of furniture necessary for the house. This mindset needs to be treated.'

Svetlana looks at me and nods as I continue, 'It all starts at home at a very young age when the boy sees how his mother is treated. That is what gives him a basic set of beliefs about the role of a woman and how she should be treated—most men come home drunk in the evening and then exhibit violent behaviour towards their wives.'

'Absolutely,' Svetlana chimes in.

'Yes, and if this is the direction our country continues to head in then we are bound to achieve only chaos. And also, the big problem is not only with our social exposure but also with our education system. We are only taught to worship science and technology when we are in school. The only purpose of education is to earn big money. I believe that it is more important to educate and enlighten the soul and the mind than to feed information to the brain. Philosophy, arts and humanities subjects need to be given more importance from an early age in our education system, across religions and cultures. That is the only thing that will make us better people and, in turn, a better society. We have a greater need for cultured, respectful minds than brains with more knowledge. Brutal and barbaric thoughts like considering having sex as a big score and something to flaunt in one's friends' circle will only grow if we ignore our age-old philosophy. Yes, we need sterner laws and harsher punishments but we cannot depend on them for the eradication of crime. We need to impart good values, ethics, spirituality and most of all, rational sensitivity at an early age with a greater focus in our schooling system. I do not see any other solution for the problem.'

Svetlana looks at me with her eyes fixed as she squints a little and bobs her head. 'That is an interesting insight, Rohit.' She turns to look at Karun and says, 'What are your views about this, Karun?'

Karun starts to speak almost immediately, 'I think the urge to commit a crime is a very basic human instinct that cannot be killed in any other way but by the use of fear. We can only stop crime in a society by making people believe that if they break the law, they will face terrible consequences. And punishments don't always need to go for death sentences. That will be like giving them the gift of mercy,' he chuckles. 'For something like a rape the guilty should be castrated publicly so that even if the rapist wants to rape again, he cannot. Men should learn to use their junk with some respect or be prepared to lose it.' He smiles and looks at the audience to see the reaction for his intended joke but most people look back at him with a straight face while a handful smile and applaud lightly.

I don't agree with what he is saying. 'But that is not . . . an evolved way of dealing with the problem. I mean sure, we must have punishment systems or things will all go haywire but that is not how we should aim to control crime. We need to eradicate the root cause and that will require introducing basic awareness and sensitivity,' I put in.

He lets out a little laugh almost as if saying *that is all bullshit* right in my face. This is really not done, I cannot take this insult.

'You know, a major problem in India is the mentality of today's youth,' I say, 'and it's everywhere. I mean, you can turn on the TV and watch a show like *MTV Roadies* and you will know it all. Half the youth population is working out in the gym trying to look 'sexy' and the other half is sitting in clubs and pubs, boozing, doping and making out. The only thing that ties all of them together is their hungry desire for their fifteen minutes of fame,' I shoot Karun a dirty look. 'Deep down inside, they know that they neither deserve that fame nor will they be able to handle it. They are impatient and irresponsible and don't want to commit to any one particular path or responsibility and that is why they are never going reach anywhere.'

'Really?' Karun shifts a bit in his chair and turns to me, 'And how do you know all this?'

'It's from my basic observations as a teacher.'

'Oh, so you teach?'

'Yes, and I think a major problem in our country is that we don't have many good teachers.'

Not everyone can become a teacher. A good teacher must be able to break concepts to such simple levels that the students can understand them. One needs a lot of patience to be a teacher, be a good listener and a great speaker and be very open-minded. At least that is what I have learnt from my experience as a teacher.

'Yes, that is a huge problem,' Karun nods. 'As we all know, *those who can, do, those who can't, teach.*'

There are a few gasps from the audience. This kid is too full of himself. He is too arrogant. I get a strong impulse to snap back and say something nasty—*you are very arrogant Karun, that arrogance only has one and only one destiny and that is doom*—but I refrain. His fate is decided, he is going break and fall one day. Holding up a mirror to him once is going to neither change nor help anything.

'What do you teach, by the way?' he asks.

'Fine arts and art theory.'

'Really? And when was the last time you made a painting or something?'

'I don't think we are here to discuss my teaching career.' I smile.

Karun smiles back. He has a look of satisfaction on his face. I want to beat him to a bloody pulp and kill him right here on the stage in front of everyone.

'There is seriously a major problem with the values of the young generation of today.' I cannot control myself. 'I mean . . . I am really sorry to bring this to everyone here but some young authors of today do anything to be successful. I know an author who used to write fake hate mails and bad reviews on every possible online bookstore just to bring the sale of the books of another author down and to demoralize him. The mails that he used to send were actually quite shocking.'

'But haven't things always been so?' Svetlana speaks up, 'I mean, there have always been some . . . bad people who go the wrong way. We have seen that throughout history, isn't it?'

I only sit there and nod. I decide not to say anything more. Already, what I have said is quite inappropriate and out of context here. I seriously need to control my outbursts. I look at Karun—he is fuming.

'Let's open this session to the audience for their questions,' Svetlana says. There is a note of discomfort in her voice. She does not seem to be particularly thrilled by the way this session has turned out.

She turns to the audience again, 'Can we have a question please?'

A boy, who appears to be in his early twenties, stands up and speaks into the mic that has just been handed to him, 'You released your new book online a week ago. The sudden release took a lot of your readers by surprise. As it was available for free, I downloaded it and read a few pages. And I have to say that I was stunned to see that the content of your book was almost directly copied from another book that came out a few weeks back. You have tried to kill a newer author by stealing his work and claiming it as your own, to gain popularity as you saw good potential in the story. I am shocked to hear you talking about values and ethics today when you yourself have plagiarized the content of your new book. I am sorry to say that it's rather hypocritical of you to talk about good values and ethics on this platform that has been offered to you.'

I want to explode. I want to shout that it was my book that was original and was stolen and published as someone else's work. I am outraged and desperate. Is there no way out of this mess? Can I never set things right and get the credit for my own work?

'I would love to answer your question but I know you won't believe me,' I say with a sigh. 'If you can then . . .'

I talk about what had happened, how my idea was stolen and I can see much support from my readers. I sigh with relief. It is enough for me that my readers believe in me.

Other questions are asked till Svetlana steps in. 'The authors will now move to the signing desk and will be available for anyone who wants to get copies of their books signed. I thank

Mr Rohit Sehdev and Mr Karun Mukharjee for gracing this event with their presence and sharing their valuable thoughts.'

~

There were several people in the queue to get copies of their books signed by me. I'm almost done now; the girl in front of me was the last person in the queue. I put a nice note with her name on the first page, hand the book back to her and get up to leave when Karun suddenly appears in front of me. What am I supposed to do with this guy?

'Quite a few people wanted to get their books signed by you. Even after all the drama that happened on stage.'

I just ignore him and keep gathering my things.

'I counted actually. A total of fifty-one people got their books signed by you. I only got a sad twenty-eight.'

'This world is not that small, Karun, that two people who don't like each other cannot find space to stay away from each other.'

He just stands there and laughs evilly. 'You know something? I think my prospects of winning the Popular Book Award this year are quite bright. The sales figures of my books are actually mind-boggling.'

'Good for you,' I say, without even looking at him.

'You know, last year, I really thought that you would win the award this year.'

'Winning that award was never my aim.'

'Of course you'll say that,' Karun laughs, 'coz there is no way you can win the award now.'

'These days, Karun, you become a bestselling, award-winning author by spending good money and devising a good marketing plan. Not by just writing a good book. But that should never be one's aim in life. It's okay if you fail to become a big author in your life, but if you fail to become a good person, then you fail everything. And right now I don't see you anywhere close to that. So it's not I who am a failure in life, you are.'

Karun looks back at me with fire in his eyes. 'You should be more careful about what you say,' he says gravely. 'It's very simple—before speaking or saying anything, just think about it a bit. Words may be wind but you never know what impact that *wind* might have on your life.' He pauses for a bit and then starts laughing, 'But maybe you don't need to be careful any more. You have already suffered the consequences. After all, your career is over. Nothing worse can happen to you now.' He smiles, 'You are *ruined*.'

'I know you wrote all those reviews and hate mails, Karun.'

'Look at you! All burning in pain! You know something? I know I hurt you. I know I wounded you. And you should be thankful to me for that *because wounds are the places from where the light enters you.* And this is a quote I posted on Facebook a few days back, by the way. You are not following me on Facebook?' He frowns, 'You should—it will help you with your spiritual growth.'

I keep quiet.

He has more words jumping in his mind that he wants to say and after a few seconds, he finally speaks up, 'That does not make any difference to me—you accusing me of sending those hate mails you got. I just wrote what I felt.' He turns around and starts to walk away as he says, 'And besides, not *all* those mails were written by me. FYI, there are other people out there who hate your writing.' Then he pauses, turns around, looks at me, 'And your guts.'

48

So he is going to get a jolt and sit down scratching his head then—Jeet

JEET OBIROI LOSES HIS 'LUCKY CHARM'

A little birdie told us that there has been a major tiff between the bestselling author duo Jeet, Obiroi and Neeti Malhotra, and they have split! The young and sexy duo who have constantly been in focus are reportedly very hot with each other in an entirely different way these days—it's only angry yelling and screaming between the duo now, which has brought an end to all the other 'hot stuff' happening between them. With the Popular Book Awards just around the corner, this was the last thing we were expecting—the duo was a strong contender for the awards. Should they win, it will be fun to see the duo receive the award on stage together—a fist-fight or a fencing match maybe? But we feel kind of sorry for Jeet—he has not written a novel on his own for a long time now, it seems, and we wonder who his 'good luck charm' will be this time? He sure needs to find one soon. In the meantime, it's a sad bye-bye to their collaboration and apart from all the novels that their readers are going to miss in the future, I am sure many will be disappointed to not see any more hot videos from them. Too bad we just got to see one. Jeet and Neeti—we wish you had shown us more!

This is utter bull shit! Who the hell is writing all this? I am going to *burn* this paper!

I pull out my phone from my pocket and call Aanush.

'Hello, Jeet, how are you?'

'Not very good, Aanush. Did you see today's newspaper?'

'I did actually.'

'Who the fuck is writing all this?'

'Even I was a little shocked to read it. I am trying to find out who the writer is.'

'I suggest you hurry up. This is damaging my image.'

'I will find out, but, Jeet, I don't think you need to worry about it much. If it's doing anything at all it's only bringing you in focus.'

'Okay . . .' I don't know what to say. There isn't really anything that anyone can do about it now.

'Take care, Jeet, I will get back to you.'

This is the most terrible way to start the day. I turn on my computer to check my mail.

```
Attn: Jeet Obiroi
    I wish to bring to your notice that I will
not be signing any contracts with you as a
```

```
co-author for the manuscripts that I have
been working on for the past few months.
I want the full intellectual ownership of
all my works and want to get them published
independently as you were not involved in
the writing process for any of those books.
    Neeti Malhotra
```

Fuck this bitch! Now she wants her books back. It was a terrible mistake to co-author all those books with her. If she takes away all the books that I wrote with her then I will lose all my bestsellers save one—the one I got published before I met her. This is trouble! I've got to do something about it. I know I'll be able to handle this, I know I will find a way to bring things back to normal and save my career. I always have, and I always will.

49

The One-Day-Lit-Fest proves to be juicer than many gossip novels, yet again—Karun

BIGGEST EXPOSÉ OF THE YEAR

Once more, the One-Day-Lit-Fest-of-the-Year has proved to be one of the most scandalous events this year. It will be no exaggeration to label what happened at the festival this year as 'the biggest exposé of the year'. It was brought to public notice that the same author who accused the owner of a renowned publishing house, Mr D.K. Dé, of cheating on the author's royalties and went ahead to accuse him of many other kinds of perversions, on and off the record, has himself stolen another author's manuscript and published it online under his own name. It was a crying shame to see the author being unmasked to reveal his hideous, monstrous side. Only a few minutes before being shamefully unmasked publicly, Rohit Sehdev was heard boasting about the great ethics and values he believes in. It is a cause for concern that such hypocritical people are the youth icons of today—who talk of great ethics and values in public but are thieves and cheaters in reality. The future of our youth seems really uncertain when the people who have the responsibility of showing them the right path are either dishonest cheats like Rohit Sehdev or perverted corrupts like Jeet Obiroi whose obnoxious sex video became viral some time back, promoting ideas as infidelity and free sex among the young people who follow him.

The only ray of hope are honest writers like Karun Mukharjee who are writing innocent and simple stories about teenagers. Karun Mukharjee announced at the festival that he will be co-authoring a novel with Neeti Malhotra, former writing partner of Jeet Obiroi, which will talk about a hot topic of our times. It sure does sound something to look forward to!

This is absolutely brilliant! I never thought it would be so easy and it would happen so quickly. Bid your writing career goodbye, Rohit Sehdev. You are completely out of the game now. What was it they say in your favourite book?

In the game of thrones, you win or you die.

You are so dead now!

50

The new boss has arrived—Shravan Kapoor

Shravan Kapoor has asked a peon to clear his father's desk so he can put his own books and things in the office. After all it belongs to him now.

Like a dutiful son, Shravan made it in time to attend his father's funeral. He performed the final rites and packed to leave the next day to go back and finish his classes. He has just another month in Prague and then he will return to India and take up the reins of the company.

There isn't any sense of deep grief at having lost his father; after all, he had never spent much time with him. And his mother is still there to provide the required financial support, which he doesn't really need any more. The only feeling he has is that of gaining something—of having inherited a treasure.

As a final gesture of respect for his deceased employer, Tahir has decided to move all of Ravi Kapoor's belongings himself—handle them with the kind of care RK would have expected. Tahir had been a constant presence during the last few days of Ravi Kapoor's life and without the filmmaker's saying anything to him in words, he had heard a lot. He knew what he craved for in the dusk of life. And seeing how blind, or rather insensitive Shravan was to his father's desires, Tahir was upset.

He had cleared up the office, organized all the belongings in labelled cartons. There were some small articles that he knew no one would value, perhaps even throw away as junk—the small paperweight in the shape of a vintage film camera; the foot-high wooden puppet hanging on a stand that had been on the table for decades. Tahir had a feeling that all these articles had stories attached to them, and he wanted to take them home for he knew that no one else would value them as much as him.

The office is empty now save for a pile of four books on the table. As he enters the office, Shravan asks, 'What's that?' pointing to the pile.

'These are the books that your father was going through. He wanted to choose one of these books and adapt it into his next film. He said he wanted to make a big film, and work on that film with you.'

Shravan looks at him for a few seconds before shifting his gaze to the books. 'Did Dad select any of these?' Shravan asked.

'I don't know, he did not tell me about it.'

Shravan looks at Tahir with narrowed eyes and then asks, 'Which one do you think we should pick up? Which one would make a good movie?'

Tahir can sense that Shravan does not like him very much, probably because of the bond Tahir shared with Ravi Kapoor. He can sense the sparks of jealousy in Shravan whenever he speaks about Ravi Kapoor with a lot of feeling and a strong sense of belonging. Given the underlying tension between them, Tahir is afraid that Shravan will do the exact opposite of what he will suggest. He is still wondering what to say when Shravan says, 'Kids these days,' and shakes his head. 'Okay, tell me which one do you think is the worst?'

Tahir knows the answer to this question. 'This one,' he says pulling out Rohit Sehdev's book. 'I think it's quite terribly written. It has no focus or storyline. It's a very confused book. But it sells like crazy. I don't know why it sells so much.'

Shravan takes the book from Tahir's hand and reads the blurb printed at the back of the book. 'You need to work on your judgment and understanding,' he tells Tahir when he's finished reading. 'This is exactly the kind of story that works these days. And that is why it is selling so much. Get in touch with the author and tell him that we want to make a movie on his book.'

'Yes, I will do that.' Tahir turns around and walks out of the office with a smile on his face.

51

At last, a few drops of happiness for her—Tara

Tara has already called up her mother in the afternoon to ask if a packet has been delivered. As soon as she comes back from college, she goes straight to her room and opens her almirah where her mother has kept the packet. Among all the gifts that Tarun gave her when he was alive, lies the one gift that he has given her after his death. The first copy of her book has been sent to her—the book that immortalizes their love for each other. Their story will now reach thousands of people. The world will sympathize with her and admire the courage with which she has embraced life.

She opens the packet and looks at her published book, *My Love Lives On*. Looking at the book gives her a sense of achievement—a kind of fulfilment that she has never experienced before. She looks up and smiles. 'Thank you, God!'

52

There is always an important reason to move on
—Rohit

This is the end of it all. Karun was right; my writing career is over. It's early morning and I am sitting with today's newspaper in front of me on the dining table and my head in my hands. They have written the nastiest story about me while covering yesterday's event. Maybe it's right what they say: there are certain desires in life that one is never meant to fulfil or achieve. They are only the fuel that keeps one going on in life, working for it tirelessly, not realizing that what one is thinking is never going happen. Maybe my desire to become a successful novelist and to be with Nisha are such desires. The only difference is that I have realized the truth of these desires and know now that they are never going come true. But I am not going to be a fool; I am not going let this destroy me. I am going to gather myself and move on. There are always enough reasons to live on around you . . . you just need to look around closely.

I put the newspaper aside, look around my apartment and

notice the mess that has accumulated over the past few days. I really need to clean this place up. My house is so cluttered that I can't even think clearly sitting here. Maybe I should start with cleaning my room. It has become so messy that it has started to smell funny too. For all I know there is a dead mouse lost and trapped in some corner of the room.

I go to my room and look around. The room is a uniform distribution of my stuff and each part of my room looks the same, just like in fractal geometry—smaller portions of mess have multiplied to create this big portion of mess, which actually has the same shape and character as the smaller portion. I decide to start with the cluttered heap of books lying next to my bed, on the floor. There are books, old and new, that I have either read or have left unfinished to read later. Among those books I find this one notebook with a green velvet cover. Looking at it my mind instantly travels back in time. This was a gift from Nisha back in the days when I had just started writing. It was my twenty-third birthday and she had decided to stay back for a while after all my friends had left once the little birthday party she had thrown for me was over. I was cleaning up the living room, gathering all the trash, when she turned off the lights and came with one chocolate muffin with one candle on it. 'What good is a birthday cake if you can't eat it all by yourself?' she had said. I blew out the candle and ate the whole muffin in less than thirty seconds. Then she took out this notebook from her bag and gave it to me. 'It's green coz it will remind you that whatever you write should contribute to a positive and sustainable society, just like the green architecture that you once studied in college,' she said.

It might sound a bit stupid but it gave me a direction to write. I had tried, I had tried to add positively to our society but I failed. And I can't really do anything more about it. I don't think I will be able to bear that kind of humiliation ever again in my life. Holding the notebook in my hands, I open it and read the note she had written on the first page,

To all the great stories you are going to write to on your way to becoming that one great author, Cheers!

I really don't know how to react to this—Nisha leaves me, then my writing career ends and then I find this notebook. *You can never forget the one you love.* You just learn to live with that vacuum in your heart that causes you a crazy pain, killing a part of you every now and then. I look at the notebook with unseeing eyes and my mind races with thoughts when suddenly I hear a song playing. It's the unmistakable tune of 'Hotel California' on a guitar. It reminds me of the day when most unexpectedly I had heard 'Moonriver' in my house and had found Nisha playing it in the living room. That was how we had patched up then. It was all so wonderful. But this is nothing like that. In fact I don't even like this song much—I quite hate it. Why do people always have to glamorize agony and drug abuse and make them into something super cool and awe-inspiring?

I go to the living room and find Pranav sitting on the sofa, playing the guitar. He's playing after ages and though I am not a fan of the song, I still go and sit next to him on the sofa and listen to him play. After a minute or so, he stops playing the song, leaving it incomplete, and puts the guitar aside. I am about to ask him to keep playing when I catch the look on his face. I have not seen him this upset before. He almost looks like he is going cry. Something is definitely wrong.

'Hey, what happened?'

'Nothing, sir-ji.' He shakes his head and does not look at me.

'Hey, come on. Tell me what happened?'

He just shakes his head in refusal. 'What is this?' he asks pointing at the green notebook I still have in my hands.

I look at the notebook and a smile creeps on my face again. 'This?' I say as turn the notebook around in my hand. 'This is the best present I have ever got.'

'Sir-ji, will you promise me one thing?'

'What?'

'That you will never be sad again. It is not nice to see you like that. I always want you to be happy. If you want, I will get you ten such green notebooks but please don't ever be sad again.'

He is being over-emotional. He is behaving like one of those characters in old Hindi movies do before they are dying or leaving someone and going away forever. Something is definitely wrong. 'Pranav, will you tell me what's wrong?'

Silence

'Look, I know something is not right. And I am sure I can help you. But not if you don't tell me anything.' I put my hand on his shoulder and look into his eyes. He looks back at me for seconds and then looks away and takes a deep breath.

'My dad called me in the morning, sir-ji. He was very angry. He got a letter from college that listed all the subjects that I had not been able to clear in the past semesters.'

'Okay . . .'

'He was saying that I have messed up my degree and I should drop out and go home. He was very stern about it.'

'Okay, but how many subjects are there?'

'It's . . . a total of nineteen subjects,' Pranav stammers.

Oh my fucking God! Nineteen backlogs? How the hell did you manage that? What did you do? Sleep all through the two years of college?

'Okay,' I force a casual, controlled nod.

'But then I called my mom. And we were able to convince him that I should get one last chance. He finally agreed on one condition. He will let me clear all my backlogs if I am able to clear my final thesis project.' He looks at me and has a hint of panic in his eyes. 'I am scared, sir-ji. What if I am not able to clear my thesis? He will take me home and never let me finish my degree.'

'Don't worry. There is still a lot of time for the finals. You can prepare. I am sure you will do great for your thesis. I will help you through. Don't worry.'

'If my sir-ji is with me then I don't need to worry about anything,' he said, hugging me.

Maybe everything does happen for a reason. Maybe my writing career came to an end because there were other more important things around the corner. Maybe I am not supposed to write because I am supposed to help Pranav, who has always helped me and been there for me whenever I needed someone. I must make sure that he does well in his thesis.

53

Love is coming back in her life—Tara

Dear Tara ma'am,

Ever since I've read your book *My Love Lives On,* I have become your biggest fan in the world. It is the best book that I have ever read. Last month I had a terrible break-up with my BF whom I had been going around with for the last five months. When we broke up I thought that my life had ended. But then I started reading your book and it gave me the courage to move on and forget him. Thank you so much for writing this masterpiece.

Your biggest fan,

Rim Jhim

Tara reads the mail and then scrolls down her inbox. It is the twenty-fifth email in the last one week. So many people have read her book. So many people have loved it. And now so many people love her. Love is something that had vanished from her life—the love of the one person whom she had loved with all her heart. But that vacuum is being filled now. She is getting love back in her life again. It's a different kind of love but it is still fulfilling. This love is coming not from the people around her or from the people she knows, but from strangers—people far away whom she has never met, will probably never meet. But it makes her happy. People like her, they love her. They think she has great potential and talent, they say that she touched their hearts. She feels more important now, more important and valuable than many other people around her.

54

The race is on—Karun

THE POPULAR BOOK AWARDS THIS YEAR—WHO WINS?

The race for the Popular Book Awards this year is getting hotter by the day. This year's awards have a bag full of surprises for everyone. As unexpected as it is, the most promising front runner of the race, Rohit Sehdev, has suddenly become the least favourite contender and seems to be almost out of the race. Apart from the other promising authors like Vikram Rawat, Jeet Obiroi and Neeti Malhotra, Karun Mukharjee and others, a new name has emerged—Tara Malhotra. Her new book topped the charts as soon as it was released and is said to be on its way to become the biggest bestseller of the year. The book is getting great reviews from one and all and has become a super contender for the awards this year. Now the question is—who will win the race? We all wait to hear the answer.

This looks good. Things seem to be going right on track but who the fuck is this new bitch—Tara Malhotra? She needs to be killed!

55

The epic smooch—Rohit

They say change is the only constant in the world and change is one thing that I am not comfortable with. I mean, just when you become comfortable with things, they alter and take a new shape and throw this new perspective in your face that you need to adjust to. I am on my way to the art studio right now and, just like in my life, things are changing on campus too. Construction workers are running up and down the corridor carrying long measuring tapes, not caring about the people walking there, almost banging into them. I myself almost banged against some of them almost three times.

'Sir-ji!'

I turn around and see Pranav jumping towards me.

'You're not going believe this! Look what I saw!' There is an unusual excitement in his eyes and he is super excited. He is literally jumping as he is flicking on the screen of his smart phone. Within seconds he shows me something that is so gross that I want to vomit. It is a picture of Jabba the Hutt smooching Megha with his mouth wide open and his head tilted to one side.

'What the hell is this!' I exclaim as I shut my eyes and turn my face away.

'Arrey, sir-ji! You don't know. This is the hottest picture ever taken on this campus. I am going mass message this picture to everyone in this college and then you will see what will happen to this fat piece of shit. He has treated us so badly for so long and now he'll pay the price with his shame. He had to some day.'

'*Are you crazy*? You can't do that!' Actually, Jabba does deserve the humiliation that Pranav wants to throw at him, so I am not going to try too hard to convince him not to do that. 'Did you really take this picture or did you photoshop it?' I take a quick peek at the screen of the phone in his hand—it does not look tampered with.

'I was in the corridor, going to the toilet when I passed Jabba's office. That stupid ball of fat—he had not even drawn the curtains of his office and he was sitting on the sofa there and kissing Megha ma'am full on. That was when I took this picture.'

'That is terrible, Pranav! Did anyone see you?'

'Hehhehheh! Sir-ji, I could give competition to Sherlock when it comes to spying.'

'Yeah yeah . . . I know.' I look around and see the workers in action wearing the bright orange jackets with fluorescent yellow stripes. 'What is happening here anyway?' I ask

'They are making some changes here, sir-ji. They are going tear down the walls of the dean's gigantic office and convert a part of it into a coffee bar where the dean can have *healthy* interactions with the students.'

'God! I wonder what kind of interactions are going to happen there. I don't know if that is a good idea.'

'Yeah!' Pranav laughs. 'What's going happen there—interactions or intercourses? Who can tell? But whatever might happen there, sir-ji, one thing is for sure—we are going to get some good coffee on campus now.'

'Oh shut up! And go to the studio now. We are going to review everyone's work today. And Jabba wants to see everyone's work too. I will just go and see if he wants to come.'

~

All the final year students have displayed their work along the walls of the studio on their easels.

I take a quick round and see that most of the students' work is fine but that of a set of four. And all four of them are gathered together and chatting in one corner. Their work is terrible. The paintings look very amateurish and unimpressive, from the strokes to the line work. Even the choice of colours is a bit disturbing. I look at the four students closely and one of their faces reminds me of something but I really can't put my finger on it. I remember seeing him somewhere with bloodshot eyes, looking almost as if he was in a trance. Somewhere . . . but where? Where—? Oh yes! How could I have forgotten! It was at the dean's pot party! In fact, all four of them were at that party. I go closer to one of the displayed canvases and squint to observe detail. What I see does not really please me. The line work is actually a direct copy of Van Gogh's *Starry Night*. The dean has been singing his song all this while about how the work of the students should be original and this is what some students are doing.

'How have the students done, Rohit?' I turn around and see Jabba walking into the studio with his characteristic walk, his feet making a terrible sound as the soles of his shabby shoes rub against the rough floor of the studio.

'It's okay. I was just taking a look.'

Suddenly, the cell phones of all the students start to beep and all of them take their phones out and look at the screen. Some of them gasp, some of them try to control their laughter, some of them giggle and some of them look at their screens, look up at Jabba in amazement and then look back at the screens again. I am certain Pranav has orchestrated this. My phone beeps as well and I pull it out to see an Instagram alert flashing on the screen. Pranav has Instagramed the picture of Jabba kissing Megha and has titled and hashtaged it '#KissOfTheSexyFatPotato'.

'Kids these days really don't have any discipline. These cell phones are a complete menace. They should be banned in this college, BANNED!' Jabba shouts.

Pranav has his phone in his hands and is smiling into the screen and typing something. Jabba notices and strides towards him. Busy messaging and unaware of Jabba's deadly approach, Pranav gets no time put his phone back in his pocket or just run out of the studio to save his life. Jabba takes Pranav completely by surprise and snatches his phone out of his hands. Oh my God! No, *no*!!! All hell is going break loose! Jabba is going be so mad after seeing that picture that we'll all spontaneously combust like that girl in the Stephen King movie!

'You are not supposed to use this in class,' Jabba says, clenching his teeth as he gives Pranav a hard look.

Pranav, foolish boy, does not apologize or look down but glares right back at him.

Oh God! Please don't let Jabba look at the phone! *Please don't let Jabba see the screen!!!*

Jabba frowns at him for a few seconds and then utters, 'Where is your work?'

Pranav simply steps aside, revealing his painting on the easel.

This is not good! This is *so* not good!

'You call this work? You call this art? A sick guy's vomit splashed on the floor looks more aesthetically pleasing than this,' Jabba starts and I hear a student whisper behind me, 'Only to you, you sick bastard, only you have a sick mind and aesthetic sense like that.'

'It looks like you have taken the shit of a sick cow suffering from dysentery and splashed it all over your canvas. Or maybe you used the canvas instead of the toilet bowl this morning when your stomach was loose and passing watery stools.'

Should I intervene? Should I try to stop his insane and sick comments about Pranav's work? I know he has put in a lot of thought and effort into this painting. Such comments can have a positive impact on no one. This is terrible!

'Your work is shit! Your work is total and complete shit,' Jabba growls and then turns about and looks at all the other students in the studio, 'All of your work is shit! You don't give a shit about your work!' he thunders. 'But now all that is going to change. You guys will have to work your asses off because now THE SHIT HAS HIT THE FAN! AND I AM GOING MAKE YOU GUYS WORK YOUR ASSES OFF!'

He looks at Pranav with even greater anger and hurls his phone back at him. Pranav catches it swiftly and both he and I take a deep breath.

'You think I don't know how you guys think? You think I don't understand your psychology? I understand student behaviour better than anyone else. I can write ten books on student psychology and they will sell *more* than Rohit's books!' Jabba bellows.

What? What the hell have *my books* got to do with this? Why the hell does he need to mention *that*? Is he crazy?

'Apart from those four students,' Jabba says, pointing at the students whose work I thought was bad, 'no one else has even a single decent stroke on their canvas. NONE OF YOU HAVE EVEN A SPECK OF ORIGINALITY IN YOUR WORK. You guys are thieves! THIEVES! THIEVES! IMBECILES! IDIOTS! RASCALS!' he screams on the top of his lungs, violently banging his hands repeatedly on the teacher's table. For a second I'm afraid he is going have a heart attack right here and die—his face has gone all red. As for what he is saying, I cannot believe my ears; I simply cannot believe what I hear. Appreciation of art can be highly subjective or relative, I understand that what is not original is not original and the work of those students is far from original.

'ALL OF YOU ARE GOING TO FAIL!' he shouts. Then he turns to look at Pranav. 'You are going to *fail*!' he hisses through clenched teeth and storms out of the studio.

It's too much to take. I need to breathe! I go and sit on the chair, holding my head with my hands and try to make sense of what happened.

'Sir-ji! Your dean has gone mad,' Pranav taunts me.

'He is not *my* dean. I mean he *is* my dean but I don't . . . like own him . . . anyway. He is just . . . stupid, I think.'

'He is not stupid, sir-ji, he is very smart. He trashed the whole class's work but that of those four students. You know why?'

'Why?' I frown.

'Coz he is guiding those four on their thesis. Even if they produce the worst paintings, they are going to pass.'

I am actually taken aback by what he says; if this is true then it is awful. But that is something I don't want to focus on right now. I have a bigger problem to solve. Jabba just trashed Pranav's work and if we don't do anything about it then there is no way that he will pass his art thesis.

'Pranav, I was just thinking . . .'

'What?'

'The dean just said that your work was trash and all that.'

'Yes. Tell me something new.' Pranav makes a face.

'What if you go to him from now on and discuss your project with him. If he gives you tips or guides you, then he cannot say later that your work is all shit because you will have done whatever he told you to do.' This is pure genius! This is the most foolproof plan ever!

56

The announcement makes him even happier
—Karun

SHORTLISTED!

The wait is over! The list of books shortlisted for the Popular Book Awards is finally out. The five books shortlisted for the most eagerly awaited Popular Fiction Award are: *The Unwanted Revolution* by Chirag Barot, *My Love Lives On* by Tara Malhotra, *And Then He Kissed Her* by Jeet Obiroi and Neeti Malhotra, *My Life, My Angel is the Best Thing in My Life* by Karun Mukharjee and *Karma is a Bitch* by Vineet Kapoor.

Let's see who the winner turns out to be this year.

Hah! This is going to be a really easy sweep. All the other books are simply trash. My novel is a sure winner. I can almost hear them announcing my name. And that asshole Rohit is not even shortlisted! I can hardly wait to celebrate!

57

**Jabba has gone blind—he cannot see the worth of
the students' work. So the spherical things in his eye
sockets should be scooped out and fed to the crows
—Rohit**

'He is a disgusting sack of fat, sir-ji, he is a spherical bastard.'

I have not seen Pranav this upset in a long time. He is clenching his fists as he is talking as if he wants to punch someone.

I am sitting in my cabin making the theory of art question paper for the term and quickly turn off the computer before he can see anything. I do not say anything and he goes on speaking, 'He had no right to say the things he said. Seriously, sir-ji, I am going to take pictures of him sitting naked on the pot and circulate them next. Shit is what he likes to talk about so much, na? Shit is what I am going to give him.'

'Will you just calm down? You are not doing anything like that. Sit down!' I pull him a chair from the next cabin; the faculty room is empty except for the two of us. It's lunch time and everyone has gone out for lunch. In fact, I was also going to leave in like five minutes but now Pranav is here.

'Sir-ji, I went to him and told him that I wanted to discuss my art thesis with him. He asked me to sit down and made me wait for a whole *fifteen* minutes as he did nothing but read some papers that were lying on his table.'

'Those might have been important papers.'

'Please, sir-ji! Don't take his side.'

'Fine!'

'After that he looked at my painting, looked at me and said that my work was nothing but the result of bad upbringing. That my mother had thrown me away like a piece of shit after giving birth to me. In fact,' he is breathing heavy again; I can see anger rising in his eyes, 'that fucking bastard said that I was the result of five minutes of pleasure for my parents and they never really actually wanted me. Because if they had wanted me, they would not have let me turn into what I have become. And then he said that he knows everything that's going on inside my head. He said that he had seen me on campus with Ramona and that the only one thing I want with her is to slide my hand down her panty. Sir-ji, is this the way to talk to a student? He has no right to talk to me like that. I have to teach him a lesson.'

'Pranav, listen to me. Calm down. I agree that he has no right to talk to you the way he did. But maybe there's a reason. You did interfere in his personal life and circulate his picture. Maybe this is karma biting you in the ass.'

'Sir-ji, it's not my karma that is biting me back, it's *his* karma that is biting *him* back—I did that because he has no right to talk to the students the way he does. He keeps saying that Megha ma'am his daughter. And then he shoves his tongue down her throat! Bloody daughterfucker! It's not me who wants to stick my hand down anyone's panties. It's him!'

'Pranav, let me go and talk to him. Let me see what the problem is. In the meantime, promise me that you are not going do anything stupid now. You are in a very tenuous position and you don't want to mess things up any more. He is the last person right now you want to offend.'

Pranav looks back at me for a while and then says, 'Sir-ji, it's only because you are saying this that I will not do anything.'

~

'May I come in, sir?' I stand in the doorway to Jabba's office. He completely ignores my presence for a good minute and then, without looking up from the papers that he has in his hands, says, 'Come in.'

I enter and stand in front of his desk while he ignores me for another minute and then says, 'Yes, tell me.' Without looking at me.

'Sir, I was discussing Pranav's project with him yesterday and I was kind of confused so I wanted him to—'

He cuts me off before I can even explain what I want to say. 'Yes, he came to me. His work is total shit. If you have been guiding him then you are the worst teacher we have ever had with us here.'

'But sir, his idea is –'

'I know what his idea is. What do you think I am—a fool? I know everything.'

He is behaving like a complete ass right now. I don't know how to reason with him. I stand there wondering what to say to him when he puts down the papers in his hands, takes off his glasses and looks at me, 'Rohit, what happens at times is that we get so attached to our students that we are not able to see the problems in their work. And sometimes some teachers are not even capable enough to guide certain students. Pranav's project is shit and with only two weeks left for the finals, I don't think he can clear his thesis. If I had known that you weren't able to guide him properly, I might have done something but now it's too late.'

Pranav was right, he is a spherical bastard—he is a bastard no matter what point of view you look at him from. There is nothing I can think of to say to him right now. I only nod and say, 'Okay,' as I leave.

Maybe Pranav was right, maybe he should have planted a bomb in Jabba's toilet bowl to explode his ass away. I am walking down to the canteen to have some lunch when I pass the final year studio where some students are gathered. Pranav comes running to me. 'Sir-ji, the marks for this week's review are out. I got only 2.5 on 10. And all the four students that the bastard Jabba was guiding got above 6.'

I go ahead and peep through the crowd at the notice board. The mark sheet is pinned on it. It has been signed by the dean.

58

Another win—Karun

'You are pure evil, Karun! And it's high time someone showed you a mirror.'

What the hell is her problem? Did she request this meeting so she could rant and rave like a madwoman and create a scene? Some of the other people in the coffee shop are actually turning around to look at us—she is *that* loud.

'You think no one is aware of what you do? That no one knows what your real self is like? Everyone knows how disgusting you are. We know that you have been sending Jeet and me all those vile hate mails. It's just that we don't want to stoop to your level and respond to your petty tactics. And I have a strong feeling that you are behind everything that has happened to Rohit.'

I only look at her. Let her vent out her feelings or she won't be able to hear what I want to tell her.

'You had no right, Karun, to announce that we are doing a book together. It's because of *you* that Jeet and I have split.'

She pauses and looks away for a moment before turning back to me. 'You are just disgusting, Karun, and you are going to pay for it one day.'

I think she has said what was pinching her the most. Now she is in a state to listen to what I have to say. 'Can I speak now?'

She only sits back in her chair and stares back at me angrily.

'I am not evil. Stop assuming that and stop believing that your truth is the only truth. There is another side of the story too—there is my truth as well. You may say that I am pure evil and the things I do are hideously insidious and despicable but that is not true. And as for me paying for the things you claim I've done? Well, we're both going to be around. You'll see for yourself that I am not going to pay for anything. Because I am not doing anything evil; I only help people and do what is good for them but they just can't see that. Just like I am doing you a favour right now but you can't see that. And about Rohit, he sucks at writing. He really needed to focus on his teaching and help his students. I just helped him to do that.'

Silence.

'These days, anonymity and obscurity are worse than being poor. Fame is the most important thing in our culture and if there is one thing that I have learned, it is that no one is going to hand it over to you just like that. You have to strive for it, you have to snatch it. If all the things I am doing are so wrong then why have wise men over the ages said that *everything is fair in love and war*? I have both the reasons to do what I do—I am at war with some people for they have been terrible to me and I do it for the love of my career.'

Silence.

'How long were you planning to live in Jeet's shadow and not have an identity of your own? I know you can write way better than him. Then why should you not get the fame and recognition that you deserve? Think about it with a cool head, Neeti; what I am saying makes complete sense. Now that you've split up with Jeet, there can be no turning back. And honestly, if you ask me, he never really valued you. For if he did, he would never have let you go . . . '

'Shut the fuck up, Karun!' she cuts me off angrily. 'What do you think of yourself? Who the hell do you think you are to tell me what I should or should not do? This is *my* life; I am not a lame puppet whose strings you can pull whichever way you want. The only reason I wanted to meet you today was to tell you that I hate your guts and you had better not cross my path again. Ever!'

She gets up and leaves.

59

When the shit hits the fan—Rohit

They are changing things around here big time. I almost don't recognize the place. The room that was previously the office of the dean is no longer his office any more—it's been shifted temporarily to what used to be a classroom so now we are one classroom short in the campus and have to 'adjust' to that. The construction workers are roaming around in the room that used to be the dean's office with giant hammers, all set to tear down the walls.

I am on my way right now to Jabba's makeshift office. He has called me to tell me something but I don't care about anything he has to say. He is a disgusting—to borrow a phrase from Pranav—'sack of fat'.

I open the door of his temporary office and just stand there without drawing his attention to me. I am determined to not say anything. If he notices me, fine. If he does not, I will just go back.

'Come inside, Rohit.'

I walk into the room and sit on a chair in front of his table. I'm not going to seek his permission for anything any more. He has lost all my respect.

'Yes, sir,' I say.

'You have been put in charge of the external thesis examination for the final year students. I couldn't help it; I tried to find someone instead of you but no one else is available. Apparently, you are our most relaxed teacher here.'

Fucking bastard! Is he trying to imply that I don't work enough? I am beating my head with students from all three batches whenever I have a free slot. I am helping the students of the teachers who don't give them the input or time they are supposed to, indirectly helping those teachers and this is what he has to say for that?

'This requires a lot of co-ordination. You'll have to prepare a list of the students, make sure the external examiner reaches on time and is taken care of It's kind of a responsibility. Please don't mess up.'

'Yes, sir.'

He looks like he's done talking. He's gone back to reading the papers on the table. I'm tempted to get up and leave without asking his permission but that will be a bit too rude, so I ask, 'Can I leave?'

'Yes, please do.'

~

It's quite a task, this thesis co-ordination. I have to make a list of all the students and cross-check and add up all the marks they have scored. Ask for and get the thesis reports submitted by each student. Check if they are relevant and explanatory enough for their project, if not, ask them to re-submit. Then send the reports to the external examiner. Follow up with him and make sure that he reads all the reports before he comes. Receive him when he comes for the exam; explain the whole marking procedure and . . . God! I am tired just thinking about it! All of this has to be done within a week and a half and so far all I've been able to do is compile the marks of the students. It was quite a day at college today. I am so tired I want to just go home and crash.

I reach my apartment and find it locked from inside. I ring the bell and Pranav opens the door. 'Sir-ji!' he greets me.

'Why didn't you go to college today?' I am so tired right now I don't even have any energy to speak. I go to the kitchen and pour myself a glass of water.

'Sir-ji, I wanted to work on my painting. I want to show that fat potato that he cannot fail me even if he wants to. I am going to create the best painting ever made.' He follows me to the kitchen. 'And then it's going to be displayed in a museum in Paris. And when all the big art critics and journalists come to interview me, I am going to tell them what a stupid asshole the dean of my college was and that he called my work shit and everything.'

As he talks, I remember how terribly low his internal marks are for his thesis. He needs to score at least 87 per cent in his external exam to pass. I walk to the living room where he has set up his easel to paint. It still needs a lot of work and I am not sure he will be able to complete the painting with the kind of finesse he will need for those kind of marks. If I have time, I will help him finish his painting the way I did last time. But I have so much work to do in the next ten days that I can't even think of doing that. And if I really think of it, is it fair to help him like that? I mean shouldn't he be marked for his own work and his own skills? But on second thoughts, his internal marks have not been what he actually deserves. So maybe helping him will not be that unfair.

'What you thinking, sir-ji? I will pass my thesis, right?' There is a strong note of anxiety in his voice.

I do not say anything. I just stand there, look at the painting and nod.

60

People are always interested to know how others fuck their love (and mess up their lives)—it's only natural curiosity—Jeet

'Hey, Jeet! How are you?' It's Aanush, my PR guy.

'Hey! I am good. How are you?'

'Good, good. Jeet, when are you announcing your next book?'

I do not have an answer to his question. Two of the finished manuscripts I had have been snatched away from right under my nose.

'I am thinking about it . . . very soon, bro.'

'Cool! All my other author clients are announcing their books and I thought I should ask you.'

'Thanks! Thanks for reminding me.' What the hell am I going to do? I need to pull up my socks now!

'Okay, Jeet, let me know when you are ready with the announcement.'

'Sure.'

'Bye.'

'Bye.' I disconnect the call.

This is awful. I have been trying to find a co-author and have got over twenty manuscripts in the past one week, but there is not even a single one worth picking up as my next book. What the hell is everyone writing these days? It's not that hard to write a novel—one just needs to think intelligently and write it. Why don't these writers understand that the whole world is not interested in their love life and how they fuck their lover? On second thoughts, maybe people always find it interesting to know how people fuck their love and eventually make their whole life miserable. Most of the literature—all the tragedies only talks about this and get the greatest acclaim.

But back to the real situation—this is depressing. I need to find a solution to this mess. The only way out of this jam will be if I win the Popular Book Award—that will catapult me back to fame and will push the book sales back up. But wait! The book that's been nominated is the one I co-authored with Neeti. Fuck! It's going to create a bigger mess if my book wins. I look at the books that I have published with Neeti and feel fury rising inside me. Why did she do this to me? All I did was put my trust in her. Just because she was not getting enough attention she decided to stab me in the back? That bitch! She has ruined everything for me. I don't fucking need her books. I have managed without her in the past and I can do so now too. I am going to give her books back.

61

And the winner is …—Karun

'And the best book award for popular fiction goes to . . .'

I don't understand why they are wasting time like this? They should just call my name and give me the award.

'Tara Malhotra for . . .'

I sit there for a few seconds, stunned. I don't understand what the hell just happened? What the fuck is wrong with them? How can they give the award to someone who has written such a terrible piece of shit? I see a girl get up on the right, look around as everyone starts to applaud and walk to the stage. She looks oddly familiar but right now I just don't care where I have seen that fucking whore before. She accepts the award, acting overwhelmed, and delivers her thank you speech, all pretentiously teary eyed. I get up and leave the hall before she can finish her stupid speech. This whole thing is nothing but a horrible shit-hole! All these awards are lobbied for. This bitch must have slept with each and every member of the jury to win this award. I need to find a better way to promote myself next year. Making sure that your name gets into the shortlist is just not enough—I will have to do more than that next year. And I will have to burn this fucking bitch down.

62

So someone thinks he needs to learn the trends
—Jeet

I need to read her book. I need to know what this *new girl* on the block has written because next year *I* need to win this award. Maybe I'll ask her to be my co-author!

The hall is echoing with the crazy applause for Tara on her win. I see her walking up to the stage on shaky legs and take the award. I don't want to sit through it any more; I know exactly what's she going to do—she is going to start weeping now and thank the whole world, naming every single person she's ever met, from her kindergarten teacher to the vegetable vendor she spoke to this morning. I get up and leave.

Enough sitting back like a lazy ass and waiting for things to get better, I need to set deadlines for myself and get back to action. I know I will be able to deliver—I have done it on my own before and I will do it again.

I pull out my phone from my pocket and dial my PR agent's number.

'Aanush, I want you to make an announcement for the media,' I say as I storm out of the building with the banners of the One-Day-Lit-Fest-of-the-Year suspended from the third floor of the building to the ground on either side of the main door.

'Tell them I have announced my next book and that it will be out by the end of next year.'

63

It's his win in her win—Rohit

She comes back with the trophy and sits next to me. She is still shaking and her eyes are full of tears.

'And with this award, we end our ceremony. A big round of applause for all the winners, ladies and gentlemen,' the host for the ceremony announces on the stage.

Everyone gets up and applauds. Tara and I get up too, and look at each other. She looks at me, raising her eyebrows, and shows me the trophy, smiling, her eyes shining.

'I know!'

She hugs me tight, I hug her back and she breaks down into tears again.

I pat her on her head. 'You deserve this; you deserve every bit of this.'

'Thank you,' she says as she pulls back and wipes her tears with the back of her hand, 'Thank you so much. All this is only because of you. If you had not helped me, my book would never have been published. This is because of you, this is only because of you.' Tara says holding the trophy in her hand. She spots someone standing behind me and says, 'I'll be right back.'

I turn around and see Nisha standing at the other end of the hall. Tara goes and hugs her and then they both scream and dance around in a circle. They both turn to look at me and Tara says something to Nisha. I look at her and nod and she nods back at me. Is this it? Is she now going to walk up to me and say that she is proud of me for what I did and that we should be together forever? Oh my God! It's happening! It's finally happening! She is coming to meet me!

~

'So?' Tara asks

'So?' I say

'What did she say?' Tara is curious.

'She told me that she is proud of what I did for you.'

'And?'

'And what?' I ask.

'Did you tell her that you want to get back together with her?'

'No.' I clear my throat.

'Oh God! Why?'

'I. . . I . . . could not gather the courage,' I stammer.

'God! Are you kidding me?'

'But it's okay,' I smile, 'I have asked Pranav to deliver a box of chocolates to her . . .'

'Okay.'

'Along with a bouquet of roses,' I grin.

'I really hope you get her back,' she says, smiling.

64

**He's in a coffee shop thinking about what he needs
to do next—Jeet**

This is better. The office had begun to feel suffocating. I am
going to come and sit in this coffee shop and write my next
book. It's a good, light environment and I see that everyone
around is happy. The crowd is lively and engaging. I am typing
the notes for a story I have in my mind when I hear someone
say, 'Excuse me, is this seat vacant?'

I look up and see a girl standing in front of me. She seems
almost as tall as me, has long hair, a slender, long neck and a
fair complexion.

'Of course, it's totally vacant.' I smile. Luck is on my side!

65

Is this the end or the beginning of a battle?—Rohit

He has done it, he has ripped Pranav's project in front of the external examiner. And Pranav wasn't able to answer most of the questions thrown at him. The fat potato asked things like 'How would you compare your painting with any painting from the Expressionist movement? Or let's say Ernst Ludwig Kirchner.' He obviously he did not get any answers. And then he goes on 'You cannot compare the two because of two reasons—you don't care the slightest fuck about Ernst or his work and no one can ever compare his work with yours because his work had a lot of depth and meaning and your work just does not have any.' Jabba is a poisonous, vicious snake—EVIL! He turns away and is leaving the examination hall now and as he passes me, he smirks at me. I want to take a knife and etch that smile permanently on his face, just like that Joker in the Batman movie.

An anxious Pranav comes running to me, 'Sir-ji! I will pass the thesis, right? They won't fail me?'

I don't say anything. I only nod. His chances of passing are very bleak. He needs to score really high to pass and from the way his viva went, I don't think he can score that high now. He is looking wide-eyed in anticipation as if I am God, as if I have all the powers in the world and only my words and verdict will be final. I look at him and feel sorry for the innocence I see in his eyes. He is going fail and only because Jabba thinks that this is his final revenge for what Pranav did. Such people should be stripped of their academic powers and banned from academia. He calls himself an academician—bullshit! He is just a power-hungry ass who wants to prove that he is in charge. He is not only ruining someone's career but is also wrecking someone's mind. How is Pranav ever going to think of him after he realizes that he failed his thesis and his dad won't let him complete his degree just because this douchebag has a personal rivalry with him. Pranav is still looking at me expectantly when the external examiner summons me.

'These students—they have no idea what they have with them. I have been trying to make them speak up but I'm really not getting anywhere. Can you please help?' the examiner looks really troubled. I look at the canvas in question: it's the same painting I had noticed the other day—the one that looks like a blind copy of *Starry Night* made by one of Jabba's students. I seriously don't want to help this kid out.

'What's he saying? I mean how is he introducing his work?' I say.

'Nothing, man, he just said that this is the painting he made for his thesis and when I asked him what his thought process was, he just stood there staring blankly.' The examiner is really irritated now. I see a few students get up and leave the room as the examiner goes on, 'I mean, this is not the kind of work I expect from a final year student for his thesis submission. It's almost an insult to me . . . I mean, man, seriously? This looks like a bad imitation of a painting done by an eighth standard student who has a bad hold on his paint brush.'

'Why don't you say something? Please explain your ideas,' I say, looking at the student who looks back at me dumbstruck.

'Actually what he was trying to do was reinterpret Van Gogh's *Starry Night*, understand all the brush strokes employed in the painting and innovate his own way to create a similar effect.' Jabba is back to defend his student.

The examiner turns around to look at Jabba and frowns. 'I think we should let him talk.' The student stands there, silently staring back at us. His eyes are kind of red. Is he on drugs? Is he stoned right now?

'He has worked quite a bit on the project actually,' Jabba defends, 'Nishal, why don't you show them your report where you had analysed the painting and all the brush strokes?'

'I don't want to see any report, I want him to speak!' the examiner snaps, giving the student a hard look. 'And seriously, sir, I don't think you should defend or support him. Please let him speak for himself.'

I walk past Jabba and smile, making sure he looks at me as I want to burn him with my smile.

~

Jabba has asked me to see him before I seal the envelope with the final mark sheet for the thesis students and submit it to the academic affairs' office. Pranav and all three of Jabba's students are failing. It is really unfair what he has done and I have never felt this helpless in my entire life. But there is nothing I can do about it.

I push the door open and walk over to Jabba's table.

'You told me to see you before I submitted this.' I show him the envelope.

'Yes, show me that.' He takes the envelope and pulls out the mark sheet. 'You see this thirty-one here?' he says pointing at the marks written in front of Nishal's name. 'Make it eighty-one.'

I nod, he smiles. I take the mark sheet, fold it and slide it back into the envelope, pick up the glue stick from Jabba's table, seal the envelope, turn around and walk away.

'What are you doing? Come back here!'

I stop and turn around. I say nothing.

'Come back here this instant and give me that envelope.' He is yelling; he looks mad like he has never looked before.

I hold the envelope up and say, 'You are not getting your hands on this. You have done enough. I will not let you spoil anything else. Just because you guided a student does not mean that the student will pass. Just because he came to a couple of hash parties at your place does not mean that he will clear his thesis by producing garbage.'

'Hold your tongue, Rohit!' he yells.

'You made me the coordinator for the thesis; I am only performing my duty. I am making sure that the marks given by the examiner are genuine and are not fiddled with before being submitted to Academic Affairs.'

'Who the hell are you to decide that? I am your boss and I'm ordering you to hand over the envelope!'

'You can do nothing to me now.'

'I CAN DO ANYTHING TO YOU! I AM YOUR BOSS!' he bellows.

I turn around and start to walk away.

'Come back here, you shit head!. Rohit! ROHIT!'

As I walk out of the door I hear him yell, 'You cannot go! I have not dismissed you yet!'

In fact, I can hear him all the way down the corridor. 'You will pay for this, do you hear me? Do you hear me, Rohit?'

I walk away with a heavy heart. This is not right; Pranav should not have failed. He actually worked hard this time. How will I ever break this news to him? Failing is not the end of the world; I need to make him understand that. Things don't always turn out the way we want them to be but that only means that we need to think of other possibilities and options. I failed to get my book published but that only made me focus on my teaching career more. We must learn to deal with our failures. Most of the time, it's more important that we succeed in what we are trying to do. My mind is churning with these unsettling thoughts as I hear the sound of loud thuds. It's coming from the dean's old office. I stop to take a look as I see construction workers carrying huge hammers and moving around. One of them is striking a wall of the office to tear it down. I walk inside the office and stand there, looking around. This is where he had sat and ruled over all of us all this while. This is where he must have made all his evil plans to fail and ruin innocent students' lives. And this is where he probably had sex with the girl he called his daughter. I am overwhelmed by the insatiable desire to destroy him.

I go to the man who is striking the wall with a heavy hammer, 'Can I do this for a bit? Can I try this hammer on this wall?' I want to tear down the wall—I want to destroy his office.

'It's not easy,' he says, looking at me as he wipes sweat off his brow.

'I know,' I say and take the hammer from him.

I strike the hammer against the wall with all my might and it rebounds, wrenching my shoulder, almost as if it hit a springboard. I hit it again and it bounces back even harder. I hit it again and a chip of the brick comes off. I hit the spot again and a crack runs through the height of the wall— brilliant light from the setting sun shines through the crevice and touches the dark floor of the room in a yellow beam of light. Again I pound the wall, and again a piece of the brick moves a tiny bit. And again and again until there is a hole in the wall. The thin beam of light grows big and the dark room is lit up. The next brick comes out easy and the next one even easier. My arms have started to ache already—I am not used to such work. I can feel the muscles in my arms, shoulder, back and chest contract. I want to use them to their full strength. I can feel the skin of my hands being torn by the rough wooden handle of the heavy hammer. But the pain cannot make me stop. It only gives me the strength to tear the wall down. The pain inside my soul is many times stronger than the pain I am experiencing in my body. I will finish this bastard. I will get him kicked out of this college. He has to pay for what he is doing. He is destroying the students' careers here. He is the reason for Tarun's death! He has to pay for what he has done in the past. I will destroy him, just like I am destroying this office brick by brick.

It's payback time!

Epilogue

When Nisha came back to see him—Rohit

I have been feeling unsettled for a long time, but things finally seem to be going the right way now. I went to meet the chancellor of the university my college is affiliated with and there was a very dramatic meeting between the chancellor, Jabba the Hutt and me. There were a lot of accusations made, a lot of throwing up of hands and angry yelling but by the end of it, it was decided that the final external examinations would be held again and this time in the presence of the chancellor himself. I think Pranav has a good chance of passing his thesis with good marks now. And the best news of all is that I have got an offer for my first book to be made into a film.

Pranav and I are cleaning up my apartment right now. It was so cluttered that I had started feeling uncomfortable and restless here. He has a scarf tied around his face and is acting like a robber, jumping from one corner of the room to another as he is cleaning it. I wish Nisha were here with me today. Life would have been just perfect. But then, nothing is perfect—it's the inevitable law of nature, so it's okay. But I know for a fact that she will always stay in my heart and I will never be able to forget her.

'Sir-ji!' Pranav suddenly taps me on my shoulder.

'What?' I say as I turn around to face him.

Instead, I see Nisha smiling and standing at the door, the light of the setting sun behind her. It's like one of those backlit scenes in one of Spielberg's movies.

I am hallucinating. I have gone mad! No! NO! This cannot be happening! I have still got so many things to do in my life! I still have so much to achieve! I cannot go mad and spend the rest of my life in a straitjacket in a mental asylum chained to a bed, struggling to free myself.

'Sir-ji, go talk to ma'am, na,' Pranav comes and nudges me.

I walk to the door and say, 'Hi!' That's when I realize that I still have the broom in my hand and I am almost shoving it in her face. Instantly, I throw it away.

She smiles, 'Can I come in?'

'Please! Yes, please!'

She walks in and sits on the sofa. I sit in front of her, facing her.

There is an awkward silence in the room for a while and then she finally says, 'I have come here to clear up a few things.'

'Okay,' I gulp.

'I know about what you did for Tara and how you helped her. I am really proud of you for that. I accused you of being selfish and not being able to think about anyone else but yourself. I take that back.'

'It's okay, Nisha, I am just glad you're back.' I smile hesitantly.

'You have earned back my respect. But if there's one thing I have learned in life, it is that people don't really change. Please don't misunderstand me; I have not come here to get back together with you. I ended our relationship on a very bad note and it would have made me uneasy if I did not clear the air. I want you to know that I don't have any hard feelings for you. We work wonderfully as friends but when we are together as a couple, we eat each other up. Neither I nor you can become the individuals we could otherwise be and shine the way we deserve to if we get together.'

I look into her eyes as she stops talking. She is waiting for me to say something.

'I do not agree with you. I know I love you. I always have and there is nothing in this whole world that I would not do to keep you happy. The irony is that what would make you happy is us not being together. Still, I will do what you want: I will never ask you to get back together with me. My heart and soul will burn with the pain of your absence, the absence of the only person in the world I long to be with but I will bear that heartache and the restlessness because, funnily enough, I know I'll be at peace, for I'll have done the one thing you asked of me. I will do this, for your happiness, to let you grow and shine the way you want to and achieve all you wish.'

So he did get his award—Karun

'And the award for the best pop fiction for the year goes to . . .' the girl in the golden dress on the stage announces, holding a piece of paper in her hand. 'Any guesses?' she asks the crowd.

Everyone applauds but no one really calls out any names.

'Yes! It's Karun Mukharjee!'

This is called success. This award ceremony has been going just the way I want it to. It's being covered by the media and the crowd is awesome. All the people from the Facebook group I created are here and they have brought their friends and relatives along. The hall is jam-packed.

I walk up to the stage to receive the award. I don't want to give a 'thank you' speech. Whatever is happening is a result of my initiative and I don't need to thank myself. I look at the audience, nod, smile and walk off the stage. One award bagged. I am famous now. Next year, the Popular Book Awards.

Acknowledgements

Thank you!

I consider myself extremely fortunate to have been associated with the people who have stuck with me through all these years of my writing career. Stories come not only from within you but also from everything and everyone around you. It's impossible to be aware of all that inspires me but there are definitely certain people whom I simply cannot forget to thank for I am very aware that without their help, this book would have never happened.

Mom, Dad, my sister and my family—I can never thank you enough but for what it's worth, thank you so much for giving me all the freedom and unconditional love that I have always dreamed of. None of this would have happened if it was not for all of you.

Vaishali Mathur, you are the dream editor any author could ever ask for. If I were to thank you for all that you have done for me and these books, it would run into several pages (or maybe a whole book). So to keep it short, thank you for your honest feedback and suggestions and your unwavering faith in my work. It's as simple as this: this book would not have been possible without you.

Shatarupa, thank you for working on the manuscript so hard and paying attention to all the details. (And I am terribly sorry for messing up all the names.) You have really helped me increase my reading speed and I think that is just super!

Bhaskar Bhatt, you have been constantly propelling my career ever since my first book. It's rare to come across friends who stick around for so long these days. Thank you so much! I think I am extremely lucky to have you around.

Rahul Dixit, thank you so much for all your help. Let's make this another bestseller!

Guneet, Aksha, Shilpa, Kunal Shweta and Ramit, your feedback (no matter how harsh it may have been at times) has always been of great help. And more than anything else, it was just your presence around me that kept me going on. Thank you so much for being there for me whenever I needed you!

Novoneel, thank you so much for always being there to listen to my frantic phone calls and for helping me find solutions to the deadlocks in my stories. Your critiques are always tremendously helpful.

Surina, thank you for all the kind words and helping me to believe in myself more.

Pavol, thank you for all the encouragement you gave after reading the incomplete drafts and listening to the broken bits of the story as I was writing it.

Akash, Shaheen, Manu, Rupal, Jaspreet, Asma, Fehma, Shagun and Arush, thank you for all the love and support. I spent some great times with you all (that gave me a lot of stories) and I am gonna remember them for a long while.

Tashi and everyone at the Tibetan Mandala Cafe, Mcleodganj, thank you so much for the many wonderful breakfasts and those great conversations.

Kuldeep, Anil, Sansar and everyone at Radha Krishan Cafe, Dharamkot, for providing me with my daily workspace.

And most importantly, I would like to thank all my readers. I would not have written any books at all if it was not for the love that I have received from you over the years. I write for my readers. There is no greater thrill in my life than to know that my readers love and enjoy my work and I strive to write good stories for all of you.

As they say, where one story ends, another story begins. Let's see where the end of this story takes the next one. So until my next book, just hang in there. Cheers!